SPARE PARTS

PARTS OF ME SERIES, BOOK 1

J. A. WYNTERS

Spare Parts, Parts of Me series, Book 1

Editing by: Sarah Villanueva at Dear Jane Editing

Cover design: Jo- Anne Walker

Interior Formatting: Dawn Lucous, Yours Truly Book Services

"This one is for Dawn,
true by name, true by nature. You spread light and joy where ever
you go."

AUTHOR WARNING

You are about to start a long journey spanning FIVE books. If you buy this ticket and board this freight train, prepare for it to be a long and bumpy ride as we delve into all the uncomfortable parts of life. These may trigger some readers so be sure you want to get on. These books will end on cliffhangers, have twists and turns and this train is sure to be derailed as it enters a long dark tunnel of depravity.

YOU HAVE BEEN WARNED.

Adult themes, strong language, graphic scenes. Enter at your own risk.

PROLOGUE

L ove is pain.

It's your bludgeoned soul and weeping heart that's left crushed to a pulp.

But love—brutal as it is—fills you up and keeps you going, even through the darkest of times. Because as much as love hurts, it's also a balm. It's a source of comfort and warmth, the place you want to rest your weary head at the end of each day.

This is a story of such love, the story of when I almost died.

How do you follow up that statement?

Well, I guess you go right to the beginning—the beginning of the end.

All the days that lead to *the* day.

The day she came crashing into my life, and nothing would ever be the same.

So how far back should I go? How deep should we delve? How much glue and tape would you like to rip away until we get to the bottom of this broken thing that I've been reduced to? How far into the void would you like to jump? The further in you get, the darker it becomes; and I am not promising you a light at the end of this tunnel. I won't even promise to hold your hand as you fall further and further into the abyss. But whether you see me or not, I'll always be there.

Let's begin.

PART I

I'm waiting for Alice, and she's sure to be late.

Alice hasn't been on time to anything in her entire life, not even her birth. The way she tells it, her mother carried her for an extra week before the doctors finally cut her out. I can't say I blame her. Maybe she knew what life had in store and she was prepared to avoid it at all costs. I guarantee that she won't be on time for her death either. She's already cheated the bastard three times, and those are just the times I'm aware of . I wouldn't be surprised if there's more I don't know about—probably best that way anyway.

This coffee is bitter, and the plastic lid leaves a shit after-taste in my mouth. For overpriced coffee, I expected better; I'm not sure why, when life has been one disappointment after another. At least there's a bit of sun today. It slices through the cold air and fizzles on my face. This bench is fucking uncomfortable, the aged wood is uneven and digs into my back. I have to keep reminding myself why I am here. I have to pretend to care. I have to latch on to that feeling, any feeling, before it vanishes like all the other emotions I've had these past months. Since it happened…

My care factor had plummeted to below zero and was

now in minus numbers. Critical mass strain. Explosion imminent.

I know you want to know why; we will get to that, I promise. But here's what I'll tell you now.

Life hasn't been easy. Despite what you may think of me at the end, remember that I worked for everything I had.

Everything.

Every tear shed and sweat wiped, every spit polish and step forward, every aching muscle and clenched fist, they were all a battle. They were all a fight for survival, a fight to get out of bed each day and face the next—where there was mostly emptiness.

Alice is now ten minutes late. I bet you she will be at least another hour. Maybe we can get through this whole thing before she gets here.

See, I know my mother.

I don't have mommy issues, at least none I care to analyse too deeply. Like I've said before, Alice isn't dead but she is mostly gone. My childhood was spent looking after the one person that was meant to be looking after me.

So yeah, I hold some resentment—a grudge even. But these days we talk once a month, and she hasn't asked for money in over a year, which I think is some kind of record. She's getting some token at the end of the month, something about being sober a while. I want to be happy for her, I do. But, the anger overshadows everything. I may forgive her one day, I might not.

For now, I still buy her a cup of coffee and a doughnut on the last Friday of each month. She was meant to meet me at ten. To be honest, I'm never really sure if she'll come. I'll give her the hour and then go. Maybe she'll show up next month; maybe her body will wash up somewhere.

On the occasions when she does show up, she tells me how well she is doing while she bites into the sweet, over-cooked dough circle. Her teeth are black, and she's lost a few on the bottom row. That gaping hole makes me shudder every fucking time.

The thing that really gets me is how her eyes light up each time she sees me. My skin crawls and itches, and I feel dirty. I want her to stop talking and her eyes to stop roaming my face, and I want to wipe her pride away with my fist.

What the hell is she so proud of? That I managed to survive her? That I managed to make something of myself despite her? Despite the midnight calls from hospitals and early morning beatings on my door begging for money? Despite the times she stole my savings or days I didn't eat.

There is so much damage—so much scar tissue to scratch and dig under—I don't have the capacity to deal with it, with her, with any of this shit.

I dig some motor oil from underneath my fingernails. My fingers miss the engine that I left waiting. This coffee is shit. Why did I take another sip? It's bitter and dark, just like my moods have been.

Well, as I predicted, she's not here yet.

I wish I'd cancelled this month. I have a full day today, and I really want to get my hands back on that engine. See, there is something pure about working with your hands. It's a sure remedy to help you get your mind off things. The harder you stretch or pull or toil and the more you clench or push, the further your mind sinks. All you see is that task before you, the challenge of metal and chrome and oil. It's a kind of peace that's difficult to acquire and hold onto. I wish I was back at the garage, sinking in hard labour.

Thing is, I don't actually need to work. Not anymore. But once you get the smell of grease under your skin, it's hard to wash off.

An engine is both complex and simple. Each part has a function, a hole, and an attachment. Everything has a place and purpose. But to complete a build, you must know the engine inside and out. You must know where each part fits, or you'll end up with something that looks complete on the outside but will never run smoothly. I should know. I am the engine my mother created. And the one person that was willing to try and take me apart just so she can put me back together? We'll get to her soon enough.

I've been fixing engines half my life. I guess you'll need to know about that—*if you're going to stick around till the end?*

Life with Alice was not pleasant, or one that involved eating a lot or often. It did involve drugs and sex. One often paid for the other. So I'm guessing that's how she met Tony, aka 'The Hand'.

It was just another day: stomach growling, cold bones, and dirty teeth. The cardboard box we slept in was crumbling around the edges, and the damp was beginning to crawl along the bottom and colour the insides black. The corroded plastic sheet no longer offered enough protection from the constant downpour. I always wondered if Alice felt the cold or if the numbness and fog she lived in made her immune to everything.

We were going on an adventure.

Alice always thought she was dragging me around Wonderland. What she never realised was that we never made it out of the rabbit hole. We just kept falling.

On that particular day, our adventures took us to Tony's. We had been there more than once. Alice and Tony had 'business to discuss.' I didn't want to know.

The very first time we walked into that place I was hit by the smell of motor oil and burnt coffee. I didn't know my cars back then like I do now. All I remember are the colours, vivid and shiny, curved and rounded in their metallic shells. Men in stained clothes leaned over or were under the cars. Tools clanged and banged as they hit the cement floor. My feet were glued in place with my back to the wall. I was mesmerised, afraid to touch any of it—afraid that my particular brand of dirt and filth would stain these beautiful beasts.

I scanned the rest of the shop and found two piggy eyes peering at me from a rounded pudgy face. From his raised office, Tony studied me then disappeared closing the curtains.

On our fourth visit, I was approached by a man. He seemed to be built of muscles. Not the bulging, overbearing ones, but the inconspicuous ones that were built for endurance and stamina. He loomed over me in his fitted suit. He eyeballed me and offered his hand.

"I'm Salvatore."

"Gabriel." I stretched out a hand to shake his, but at the last second he pulled it away and ran it over his jet-black hair. Heat prickled my ears as a smile spread across his lips.

"Follow me." He turned on his heels and led me to a small kitchenette tucked away at the left-hand corner of the garage.

My stomach churned and growled, probably because I was in a kitchen, but most likely because it had been a few days since I had last eaten.

"Sit." Salvatore shoved my shoulder and I fell into a white, plastic chair. It was too big, and a red, sticky substance attached itself to the back of my pants. The fabric hissed as I pulled my leg away. "Boss wanted you to have this."

Like a magician, Salvatore produced a sandwich and placed it in front of me. My mouth frothed and my stomach clenched. I sat staring at the bread, a slice of cheese mocked me from between the slices. My hands sprang to the bread and gripped the sandwich somewhere between a death grip and the most delicate touch I could muster. The first bite was heaven. A sharp tang of mild cheddar sliced through the dry, yeasty bread. I demolished the first half in seconds. I should have savoured it, but that's like telling a cat to take it easy on the mouse it just caught.

When you're a kid you shouldn't have to be sensible. It's not built into your DNA. You should be asking for chocolate three meals a day, jumping off tall shit and hurting yourself on a regular basis. In my case, it was be sensible or die. I know it sounds dramatic, but it's true. Spend ten minutes with Alice and you'll get what I mean.

Halfway through that sandwich, I stopped cold. I held the food an inch from my face and forced my hands to pull away. Forced my stomach to accept that that's all it would be getting. Forced my mind to accept that, if we could just hold on a little longer, we could eat the rest later. Later.

Later would be better.

With agonised movements—sinew fighting muscle, bones fighting tendons—I inched the sandwich away from my mouth and tucked it into my pocket, wishing I had something to cover it in.

"What the fuck are you doing?"

I jumped in the seat, my heart leaping into my throat. In my food coma, I completely forgot about my guardian. I was so used to being invisible.

"I'm... I'm... I'm saving it for later." I focused on a glossy red spot on the floor.

"Why?"

"Because I'm hungry." My voice cracked and my ears burned, but my eyes remained on the drop of jam. My mind compartmentalising—humiliation to the side, task to the forefront. How to retrieve fallen jam: A swipe of the finger? A lick of the tongue? A wipe of the bread against the floor?

A muted thud interrupted my thoughts, and I looked up at the source. Salvatore had slammed an almost full loaf of bread in front of me.

I searched his face, looking for the usual looks—pity, empathy, maybe some compassion. But all I saw in his stormy, blue eyes was anger. "Eat the fucking sandwich, kid." He stormed out of the kitchen.

Food and heat became motivators to go to the garage. I

started hanging around even when Alice didn't take me. As usual, she would disappear. Sometimes for days.

The men pretended like they didn't see me, until one day someone needed a spanner, and a socket wrench and then maybe I could hold something or start a car, or pop a hood.

Tony's piggy eyes followed me around the shop. Maybe if I had met him earlier, I would have never come back. My path would have led to a gutter next to Alice. But hey, a gutter is still better than where I ended up.

I can't give you exact days or times. As a kid, time isn't really important. You look forward to events, and you have an idea of when these events would be coming up. To most kids, this would mean a birthday or Christmas. You could ask how many months, then weeks, then days, and you would count down. The only real idea to hold on to is you slept and woke up, and that meant time had passed.

In my case, I counted time by when I would eat, or when Alice would come back. Or when it would rain, or when it was cold or stopped being cold. I had no Christmases or Halloweens, there were no birthday parties or celebrations. Just survival.

So, I can't tell you how much time passed before the day Salvatore called me into the kitchen.

Since that first day with the sandwich, I had free reign of that kitchen. All the men pretended like the extra loaf of bread and occasional chocolate were always there. So, when Salvatore guided me into a plastic chair, my stomach coiled and cold pins slithered beneath my skin. I scolded myself for eating the last of the bread. I should have saved it, not become complacent. My lip quivered, but Salvatore cut me off before I could start begging.

"You like coming here kid?"

"I... I..."

"Do you want a job?"

"A job?" I peeled my eyes away from my worn shoes and

searched his face. His dark-blue eyes met mine. Salvatore was not a soft man. He was all hard lines and jagged edges. But he had a kindness in him that he chose to share with me. Maybe that's why he stuck around so long. Maybe, in the end, it's why I adopted him—because he adopted me first.

He nodded.

"What sort of job?"

"Just running errands, helping the boys in the shop, and whatever the boss asks of you."

"Will I get money?" My fingertips twitched with the idea, I would be rich. Anything more than zero was already a step in the right direction.

"No."

"Oh." My disappointment was palatable.

"But," my body righted itself at the word, my ears pricked up, and I leaned forward in my chair clutching the table. "You will get a place to live and food. Everyday."

My mouth fell open as I tried to digest the idea of stability. My mouth dried up as if my eyes had sucked all the moisture from my body, and tears pooled behind my eyelids. "Every day?" I shook my head as if I hoped the idea would sink deeper, if I just believed it enough.

"Come with me." Salvatore's face didn't move, not a twitch or a tremor of any kind. His voice remained flat and unconcerned, but his eyes gave him away.

I followed him out of the kitchen and along the wall of the workshop to the door on the right. It had always been sealed, and a fading sign that stated 'Staff Only' clung to it.

Salvatore pushed the door open.

The room was narrow. Two metal shelving units leaned against the wall, the over-stacked shelves strained and dipped with effort. A layer of blue dust covered every surface. We stepped deeper into the room. Dirt particles flew like fairies into the air and danced in the shaft of light coming from the window.

Salvatore pushed open a second door. Peeking into the room, I saw a toilet and basin. Both were layered with dust and smelled like mildew that had saturated into the porcelain —pungent and sour.

I stood rooted in place scanning the small room.

"We'll clean it up." His stony voice boomed off the walls. But I didn't care. I didn't care about cleaning the place or moving the shelves or wiping the toilet. I would have a roof and a heated place. Permanently. I wanted to run into his arms, to let him cradle me as I wept into his shirt. Instead, I nodded and wiped at my eyes.

This was the best day of my life.

I didn't know it then, but it was also the worst.

I never really questioned why Tony 'The Hand' Albertelli took pity on me. Chances are, he was pimping out my mother and needed me out of the way.

Either way, that bacon-smelling grease monkey taught me everything I knew about cars, bikes, and cold meats. The man loved his sandwiches almost as much as the garage. Some called it a chop shop, but it wasn't really that. Sure, there were the late-night disassembling of vehicles and disposing of parts. But in reality, the shop was legitimate—a legitimate money laundering operation.

Much later, after everything happened and I bought the shop, all that illegal stuff stopped. There was a price to pay, a buy out if you will.

See, I figured I have lived in a prison all my life. I was a prisoner of hunger and suffering, of loneliness and desperation, of circumstance and childishness. In adulthood, I wasn't going to owe a damn thing to anyone. Not a single mother-fucker. I would pay my debts and carve my own way under my own terms.

I was never going to be held prisoner again.

Back then I was naïve, thinking that if I just did the right thing and paid my debts it would all be over. No more prisons, no more walls. I was an idiot. But then again, aren't we naïve before we fall in love?

Love. A prison of your own device. Cracked, grey walls that keep out the light and sound. In the stillness and darkness you could lose yourself completely, disoriented by the design, your soul a suffering agonised inmate.

I was fucked.

Locked up.

Chained down.

And totally lost.

Thinking of her, that very first time we met, still makes my spine shiver and my skin crawl. My life changed the minute she walked into it. A point of no return. A veritable fork in the road.

But we'll get to that.

To her.

Even thinking of her gets me all muddled up, and here I am trying to keep all my ducks in a row, to tell a singular story in the most linear of ways. You'll have to excuse me. Just the thought of her tugs me in all directions.

As I was saying….

'The Hand' was not a good guy, but he was a good teacher. About a week after I moved in, he finally summoned me up to his office.

His enlarged body spilt over his sagging chair as his piggy eyes pierced through me. With a single sausage finger, he bid me over.

All people give off a smell and, whether or not we are aware of it, our noses catch it. It is a singular and particular odour that each human wears that feeds our instincts. It tells us if we should be attracted or repelled, enchanted or repulsed. In Tony's case, it told me I should be petrified. He had the smell of a predator, of something that could hurt and maim—not kill—just enjoy the pain of others. Cold liquid ran up my spine. My legs turned to jelly as I forced myself nearer the danger.

"So, you're the kid?"

I nodded, uncertain. He reached for my face, his fingers clasped around my jaw. Tony examined me like he would a horse. Turning my head in all directions, pulling at my hair, searching for lice, prying my mouth open. He didn't look at my teeth, just ran a finger along the base of my tongue, pushing it until I gagged. He smiled, I shivered.

"Do you like your new home?"

"Yes, thank you."

"Good. Your mother and I came to an arrangement."

I waited for more. There was always more.

"The boys will stay after work today and help clear out that room. There's a bed coming, and I have a guy that will fit a shower head for you. We have to keep you clean if you're going to work for me."

"Yes sir."

A crooked smile stretched across his face, pulling the sagging cheeks. "There is only one rule here, Gabriel."

He nodded to Salvatore who approached us from the door. Without warning, he grabbed my wrist and spun me around slamming me against the heavy, maple table. With a huff, my lungs emptied of air and pain shot through my abdomen. Salvatore twisted my arm, pulling and pushing it against my back, the pain screaming to my shoulder. He tugged, I cried out.

Tony leaned against me, his chair groaning beneath him. His hot breath in my ear, a hint of peppered salami coated my upper lip.

"All you need to do is do as you're told, and keep your mouth shut." Salvatore tugged at my wrist, and I yelped with the pain.

"Do you understand?" Tony's voice was even and unperturbed.

"Yes sir." I managed through gritted teeth.

"Good." Tony's form moved away, yet Salvatore did not release me. He held me like a rag doll, adjusting the pull on my shoulder and the angle of my wrist. I whimpered, the hand around me tightening.

Black stains tainted my vision, and my breathing grew heavier. I concentrated on the table, the film of dust and coffee mug rings, the delicate grain of the wood, a blue pen. I sucked in breath and yelled. The effort of filling my lungs pushed against my rib cage, forcing my shoulder to move. I could see the black, it was coming and with it would come relief.

"Let him go." In an instant the grip around me relented, and my body slumped unsupported to the ground. I sucked in lungfuls of air, rolling my aching shoulder. "Get him out of here. We all have work to do."

Salvatore's strong arms reached for my shirt, and he yanked me off the floor. Our eyes met for a split second and in it, I realised that I was all alone. Maybe in the turbulent water of his eyes I was looking for an apology, empathy, or remorse. All I found was a gaping, endless, dark hole.

He shuffled me out of the room and into my new life.

PART II

That first year I was running errands for him, and he gave me a bed and threw food my way. The man ate enough for six people. Food was a commodity I was happy to trade. To be honest, I was grateful. I was too short and too skinny for my age; my skin was unhealthy and my hair thinning out. The other benefit? My mom never tried to steal my food. All I had to do was keep my head down and mouth shut.

I had been working at the shop for close to a year, and maybe that's how long it took to prove your loyalty to Tony. It's not that I ever felt like he was testing me, but I had eyes and ears. And even with the little education I had, I knew everything that was going on.

Everything.

All I had to do was keep my mouth shut.

Sealed.

Vaulted.

I just wanted to eat and stay warm and safe. You would have done the same.

The Hand called me into his office. He sat behind his desk, a red ketchup stain smeared the collar of his shirt that pushed up around his pudgy neck. His face was peppered with meat sweats and he wore a crooked smile.

He waved me in and offered me a seat.

"Gabriel, my boy. Happy birthday." He pushed away from his chair and popped out of it like a Champagne cork.

"It's my birthday?" My heart fought the sensation of caving into itself. Joy marred with pain.

"Sit." Tony pointed at the chair across from his table, then proceeded to open his top drawer and pull something from it. He rounded his table, carrying the plate.

My eyes watered as he lit the single candle on the slice, and I remember the tears stinging my cheeks. I couldn't unglue my eyes from that flame as it got closer and closer. He was heaving by the time he shoved it in my face and was bursting at the seams. Tony told me to blow.

I must have looked a sight. A sorry skinny thing, a burbling crying mess over a single piece of cake. He pretended that he didn't notice the tears, that my pain didn't smash against the walls of his office and that my joy was ordinary.

I wondered if he knew it was the first cake anyone had ever gotten me for my birthday, and one of the few birthdays that had ever been celebrated up to that point in my life.

My mind shot to Alice, and the one time she took me to a restaurant. She was dressed in her best shirt and short jeans that were shorn on the bottom. Her handbag dangled from her bony shoulders and she led us inside. She'd been promising me a burger on my birthday for days and when she woke me up that day to celebrate, I jumped through my skin. She licked the stains from my face, and we left the house. At that time, we were staying with one of her friends. We were allowed, as long as he didn't see me. The feeling was mutual. I remember standing at the door, the smell of cooked meat and oiled chips ripped through my stomach and made my mouth water. And I remember how she shouted at the man who didn't let us in. She screamed at him and shoved money in his face. And I remember the eyes—so many eyes looking at her, at me.

I shook away the memory. Tony let me finish my sniffling and swept all my emotion under the table, asking me to eat. In truth, I had no appetite. I was too overwhelmed but refusing was not an option.

That first bite was an explosion of sweet on sweet. Vanilla and chocolate danced on my tongue, delicate creams and crunchy biscuits, flaky chocolate and buttery sponge. It was heavenly. The most exquisite thing I had ever tasted, and I wanted it to last forever. I wanted to savour that slice, as much as I wanted to devour it.

The Hand watched me eat, licking his lip with each of my mouthfuls, sweat rolling down his face, plummeting into the depths of his neck coils.

I put the empty plate on his desk, thanked him and was getting ready to leave.

"Gabriel, can you read?"

A hot flush crept along my cheeks at the question, the sweet cream of the cake soured in my mouth. "A little," I mumbled, my hand curled around my middle.

"And math?"

"I know numbers."

"Can you add?"

"Some." I looked at my hands, the bony fingers rubbing against one another.

"Well, that's just not good enough."

In the silence, I could sense his impatience growing. My eyes shot to his face and he continued. "If you are going to work here, you need to know how to read and write and how to add numbers and do math. We have inventory to take and parts to order, there are books to be kept and people to deal with, and if any of those people even get a sniff of your lack of ability, they will try to find a way to fuck you around."

He took a long breath in and hissed it out. "I don't like getting fucked around."

"No, Tony." I nodded.

"You need to go to school."

I opened my mouth to interrupt, but he held up his hand silencing me. He knew all my objections even before I named them.

"You will earn your schooling, in the same way that you have earned your board and food. You will work every day after school, and you will continue to keep your mouth shut."

I remember vaguely feeling faint. Petrified. I know I should have felt grateful, but school meant so many things I couldn't fathom. To begin with, other kids; kids that ate, and had money, and probably knew how to read and write.

Then, there would be the pressure. What If I could never really learn? What would Tony do, if after a few months, I still couldn't spell or add? How would I do homework and shop work? My mind collapsed in on itself.

I don't remember speaking or protesting, crying or fighting. But I do remember Tony declaring the case closed.

He told me school started in a few months and, until it did, I would have a tutor coming to the shop three times a week to teach me the basics.

I stumbled out of his office. Gloom clouded the rest of that day. At the time, I didn't realise the magnitude of the gift Tony gave me. Sometimes I wish he was still alive, so I could thank him properly. But not often. That son of a bitch is best on his back six feet under.

The rest of the summer I worked like a dog. Hell, I wasn't much better than a dog. I was often dirty, fed in rations and often slept on a mattress harder than the floor—and I was scared. I didn't have to be on a leash to be scared. I felt trapped, I owed him.

There was a lot of backbreaking work. You might laugh about it today but for a scrawny fourteen-year-old, packing boxes full of parts and hauling mystery boxes into the night, was hard work. Backbreaking.

But then, I met Rita.

Rita was my tutor and my first wet dream. Not at first, but later and frequently. She was tall for eighteen and blonde; the kind of lush, shiny hair rich girls had, the kind that smelt artificially fruity and clean.

She had a thing for those high sweaters—you know those that stop well above the belly button—and jeans that were torn around the knees. She was the right kind of sexy. Not slutty, not in your face—just confident.

Of course, with me, she was like a big sister.

At first.

She showed up at the garage every other day at four o'clock. She was never late and never unprepared. I guess that's why Tony picked her.

He gave us his office for an hour and a half and I have to admit, I surprised myself. I wonder if I progressed so quickly because I was actually smart, or because I was afraid of letting Tony down. Maybe I was just trying to impress Rita. Really, it doesn't matter. In a month I was reading fluently. I started with words like cat and hat, progressed to thunderous and instantaneous, and calamity and monumental.

In that same month, I could suddenly see numbers in my head. Ones and twos added up and then hundreds and thousands. Math made sense and, all of a sudden, I was privy to a whole new world. A world I didn't know existed. A world of books and words, of intellects and storytellers. It was beautiful, it was magical, and I'm pretty sure, it saved my life.

At the end of that summer, Rita and I parted ways. She gave me a peck on the cheek and told me how proud she was of me.

My cheeks burned and my stomach coiled. I realised I would miss her.

A week before school started, Tony bought me two sets of

uniforms—summer and winter. In no uncertain terms, he explained they would be the only ones he would purchase.

They were my prized possession and my responsibility.

The night before my formal education began, I barely slept. The hard bed felt like a log floating on a river bed. And no matter how much I tossed and tried, there was no comfort, no warmth. My mind was plagued with thoughts of Alice, of the future. The shop creaked and moaned, metal squealed and the darkness bore down on me as I sweated and shivered.

That first day of school was one of the scariest days of my life. It was worse than that day I found Alice blue and foaming at the mouth. Because losing her would have been a relief. Death was final. School was going to last for four long, torturous years.

I was picked as a target the second I stepped foot on the stairs of that damn school. I mean if I was Archie Bolton, I would have picked on me too.

He smelt like money, like laziness that came with having everyone doing the hard work for him. His mouth was tinged with the scent of the silver spoon he's been sucking on, and his clothes were sewn from entitlement.

And me? I didn't belong in this place and he knew it, just as much as I did.

My hair was all kinds of wrong, unruly and undisciplined. My body didn't fit the uniform that sagged off me, like old skin that grew too weary of its bones.

I can go into great detail about those four years, but I won't. Because, that's not why you are here. I will tell you about the only four significant events you do need to know about.

The first? Despite what you might think, Archie didn't lay a hand on me. He tried, that fucker. I was small, but damnit if I wasn't feisty. To survive on the street, one must pick up a set of skills that ensured you did just that—survive. A spoilt fucker like Archie only knew how to swing a fist. He didn't know how to eat one. He also didn't know how to defend himself against low blows. He was an idiot, thinking I wouldn't use them. After that first beat down, that asshole didn't come within a ten-meter diameter of me. On the first day of school, I spent half of my lunch break in the toilet washing blood off my blazer. He was cowering in the courtyard behind his friends and his father's money. Turns out that his father's money didn't reach as far as Tony's.

Archie Bolton never came near me again. He barely acknowledged my existence. I, in turn, did the same. Not because I wanted to. I wanted to break that fucker, tear him limb from limb, and rearrange that precious face of his that was always so meticulous. Yeah, Archie Bolton didn't touch a hair on my body.

But Salvatore did.

At the end of my first day of school, Tony summoned me to his office. His round face pink, and his eyes sunken under a furrowed brow.

"First day of school and you're already getting into trouble?" His voice was sharp and low, and a chill ran down my spine.

"But Tony…"

"Grab him." His eyes flickered to the wall, and in seconds Salvatore lunged at me and had me in his grip. I struggled against him and he held me as if I was nothing but a wisp of smoke.

"Hold him down."

Ever the obedient soldier, Salvatore dragged my flailing body over the table. With my wrists clasped in his hand, he pushed at the small of my back, forcing my upper body against the wood.

"Tony, please—I…"

"Do you know how much I had to pay to get you into that fucking school?"

From the corner of my eye, I could see his large shape moving. His chair moaning as he stood up. I pulled against Salvatore's grip, but it was like fighting steel. "Tony, I'm sorry…" I pleaded, but he ignored me.

"Do you know, little boy, how much I had to pay to keep you in that fucking school?"

"Tony…" the words choked in my mouth as a pair of hands reached for my pants and yanked them off my body. Cool air tickling my ass and balls as they hung exposed . My heart pumped wildly as I tried to no avail to thrash and fight against Salvatore's iron grip. "Tony, please…" I could feel tears as they fell across my nose. My cheek chaffed against the wood.

I yelped as the heavy belt left my buttocks, the sting sharp crackled against my skin.

"You have one job boy."

The belt licked at my skin with force. I thrashed against the table to no avail.

"Head down."

CRACK.

"Mouth shut."

The belt slapped against my skin.

"One fucking job."

With that, Tony clamped his mouth and let his belt do the talking instead. The blows rained down on my back and bottom, legs and calves. I gritted my teeth as tears leaked from my eyes. With each blow, the skin softened and the pain grew until my entire body felt as if it was on fire.

"Do you understand?"

The strikes seized just as quickly as they had begun.

"Yes," I whispered through gritted teeth and foam, through balled fists and choked breath.

"Good. This will be your only warning." He coughed and Salvatore released me. I wished he hadn't because he was the one thing that was holding me up. I clawed at the table but the smooth surface had no grip, so I slid and staggered backwards into the wall.

"Get dressed and get the fuck out of here." Tony's voice was breathy and his chest heaved. His pudgy hands fumbled with the belt trying to push it back in through the loops.

I pulled up my pants, the fabric stinging my welted skin. Salvatore led me to my room and laid me on my bed.

For the next few weeks, my body would hurt. The welts turned from an angry red to blue and black and eventually yellow and purple.

It was a harsh lesson, and I obeyed. Head down, mouth shut. I wished I had let that asshole, Archie, just beat me up instead.

The second thing that you need to know is not an event, but rather a fact. Turns out, I was super fucking intelligent. Who knew, right? Yes, Rita gave me foundations—and good ones. But once I got started, I realised that I had an appetite for knowledge.

I had always been street smart, I had to be with Alice. I wasn't stupid. I knew what was going on, but it was only once I was educated, once I understood the complexity of numbers, that I comprehended the depth and ingenuity of how Tony's business ran. The cleverest thing? Tony kept his name off of every single slip of paper in that joint. It's like he didn't even exist.

I spent the days at school and the evenings at the shop. The quicker I absorbed things at school, the more Tony taught me about the business. All sides—the good, the bad, and the right down dirty.

Which leads us to number three. I wasn't just smart, I was athletic. And because I was getting fed regularly, I buffed up. My growth spurt happened almost overnight. The scrawny kid vanished, and in his stead was a healthy strong teenage boy. I suddenly had muscles and sloping shoulders, a broad chest and long powerful legs. I became strong. I was strong.

Football came naturally to me. Like the ball was an extension of my body. Like my legs were designed to run, and my upper body was created to clash and force its way forward.

I wanted to play football. In fact, coach wanted to recruit me. He filled my head with dreams. He talked about universities and scouts, about draft picks and a future.

The Hand laughed at me when I mentioned it. I remember the spittle as it flew out of his mouth. It was heavily scented with salami fat and bread crumbs. His small eyes squinted almost shut, and his hands fell onto his rounded belly.

That fucker laughed.

Tony dangled the dream carrot in front of my face and tore it away with the same hand. The Hand giveth and he taketh away. That day, as his body giggled while he nearly fell over with hilarity, I understood the price of his gift and the debt that was owed. I was being groomed to be his, and his I shall remain. I was his prisoner. The walls sealed around me, the gate slammed shut. I was never getting out.

When I stopped showing up for practice, coach tried to speak to me, motivate me, shower me with praise. I told him it was never going to happen. He slapped me across the back and promised he would make it happen, assured me he had never failed to convince a single parent to give their kid the best start in life.

He strolled right into the principal's office.

When he came out, he could barely look at me.

"Don't worry about it." I slapped him on the shoulder and left him in that corridor looking at his feet.

And number four?

That happened two years before I graduated. Rita came back. She sauntered into the office, all sweet and rosy. Her blonde hair was swaying behind her in a high ponytail. She looked like a prized horse. It swayed and sashayed as she moved.

I watched her. It was like seeing her for the very first time. I found it hard not to notice that her lips were a dark shade of red, deep maroon, all glossy and shining as the tip of her pink tongue sailed across them. I noticed how her sweater hugged her midriff so tightly that her breasts had nowhere to go but up. They bobbed ever so timidly with every step she took. Her high heels clacking on the concrete floor.

Rita didn't even turn her head in my direction. The likes of her didn't associate with us grunts. Bottom feeders.

The help.

She crossed the shop as if she was afraid to catch something. Quick enough to get out of the dirt, but slow enough to make sure every male on that floor looked. All got an eyeful of what we could never have. Turns out, Rita was Tony's niece. Who knew an ugly sack of shit like him could be related to her?

Not long after she went into the office, he called for me.

I walked into the office and caught sight of her long legs peeking from her black mini skirt. My body tightened and I swallowed hard. I averted my eyes and found Tony's burning with anger and warning. I straightened up.

"You need something, Tony?"

"Gabriel my boy, you remember Rita?"

I nodded and shifted my attention back to her. I could see her eyes widen and her nose flair as recognition set in. Barely.

"Gabriel?" She sucked in a breath trying to conceal her astonishment. "What happened to the scared scrawny kid?"

"Your uncle fed him." I shrugged and she giggled. The sweet sound forcing its way to my pants.

"I can see that." She said in a playful voice and raised an eyebrow.

"Rita!" Tony's tone held no questions as to his disapproval

of our exchange, but Rita ignored her uncle. And winked at me.

Although my body reacted, I kept a straight face.

Tony turned back to me, "Rita here pranged her car." He crossed his arms and they rested over his belly. "She is going to borrow the Lexus until we can fix it up for her. Make sure you get her the keys. You will need to pick up the Mustang. Rita here will drive you to it."

"Yes sir."

The three of us remained silent for what seemed like a minute. "Was there anything else, Boss?"

"No, get out of here, both of you. I have work to do, and I'll have even more work if the cops find her car first."

Rita stood up and tottered over to her uncle pecking him on the cheek. He turned a shade of crimson, and I could see the dirty thoughts churning in his head. She was his niece. My stomach churned.

I turned away as she said in a sweet voice, "Thank you, uncle Tony. I knew you could help me."

"Anything for you, sweetheart." His voice was soft and rosy, completely unrecognisable. I wanted to vomit.

I held the door open for her, my knuckles white on the doorknob. Her soft fingers grazed my hand as she exited, my breath caught in my throat as I slammed the door behind us. Rita flashed me a dazzling smile as she waited for me at the top of the stairs.

"Follow me." I took a wide step around her and led her downstairs and to the back. The storage room was dim and hot, and my heart thumped with every click of her high heels behind me.

"Through here." I waited by a wall. To the naked eye, it looked like a regular wall. But in reality, it was a false wall hiding Tony's real treasures.

In the hidden room was a garage where The Hand kept his cars. And where more than a few nefarious jobs had taken place. The place was spotless, bleached and immaculate.

"Stay close."

There were rules, everyone knew the rules, even those who pretended they didn't. The room had to remain in complete darkness until the door was firmly back in place. The outside world could have no idea about the existence of this place. Not even the light was allowed to leak out.

I unlatched the hidden door and stepped inside; Rita did the same. She remained close, and I found it hard to swallow.

"I have to close the door, it will be dark for just a minute." She nodded at me and shuffled closer still. I could feel the heat of her body inches from mine.

I slid the door into place. The world plunged into darkness, and then I could feel her hands on me. They clawed at my chest and wrapped themselves around my neck. I sucked in a breath.

I slid my hand along the cold wall, searching for the light switch. Rita pressed herself against my body, the feel of her breasts against me sent my mind reeling. My heart pounded in my sixteen-year-old chest.

In the darkness, her smell intensified. She smelt like a field of lilies, like she rolled around in the petals. I could almost picture her nude body being stroked by each flower as they kissed her skin. The bulge in my pants became tighter, and I could feel the sweat on my forehead as my fingers finally found the switch. I stood frozen in place.

I could feel her hot breath on my chin, and then my cheek as she pushed herself up on tiptoes. I was completely unprepared for the feel of her lips on mine. For the heat of her tongue as it swept past my lips. For the path her fingers forged along my back and into my hair.

The kiss only lasted seconds but it also lasted an eternity. Universes were created and worlds ended during that kiss.

My body was hard and tight in all the wrong place, and my lungs forgot how to breathe.

"Mmm Gabriel," her voice was husky and my body coiled. "You best put the light on."

I nodded like a fool at the total darkness, and the heat of her body melted away.

The room exploded into harsh light. White walls and black cars and the pink, sweltering flesh of Rita as she stood inches from me.

I stumbled backwards and my back hit the wall. A smirk spread over her lips as she unashamedly scanned me, her eyes making the journey down then up again. She bit her lip and turned away, the clack of her heels echoing in the cement chamber.

"Which of these is it?"

"The Lexus. Far right." I cleared my throat hearing the strain in my voice. "I'll grab the keys."

I fiddled with the flimsy latch on the key box and grabbed the ones for the Lexus, dropping them and picking them up again. Rita snickered. My world had just been slanted, tilted, and she knew it.

It's not like girls hadn't made passes at me before. It's not like Elaine didn't let me feel up her boobs behind the bleachers at the football field, and it's not like I haven't been kissed before—more than once. But this was somehow different. She was older and pretty and I knew her. She didn't look at me like I was a piece of shit, like she was a rich girl coming to slum it down with the grubs.

She looked at me like I was just another boy. And that was enough—not different, not extraordinary, not poor. To her, I was just like everyone else. It was enough to make my legs shake and my heart thump. Well, that and her bloody perfume, and that midriff of hers—showing off soft flesh that jutted out, winking at me, teasing me, daring me to touch it. My sweaty fingers itched for it.

I unlocked the car and opened the door for Rita. "A gentleman." She smiled at me.

If she knew the wicked thoughts that ran through my brain, I don't think she would have called me anything more than a beast. I just smiled back and climbed in the driver seat. My hands clutched that wheel so tight my knuckles were all kinds of white.

"Where is your car?"

She gave me the address and I put the car into drive. It glided out of the parking bay and through the tunnel. Soon we were on the street.

The sun bathed the buildings in golden-orange light as if the city was burning as hot as my skin. Dark blues chased the sun, forcing it below the horizon. Soon it would be dark.

We drove in silence for a while. My hands started to relax; my body fell back into the driver's seat, easing against the comfortable leather. But my skin remained prickled, acutely aware of her. I felt like a match in a lightning storm. A single touch was all it would take to ignite a wild, hungry fire.

"You've grown." I could feel her eyes on me.

"It happens." I shrugged, pretending that I didn't like that she'd noticed.

"And filled out."

"Your uncle pays me. I can eat now. Every day." It was sarcastic, and I kicked myself for being such an asshole. There was a beautiful girl saying beautiful things, and there I was being a dick. Let's call it self-preservation. I could still taste her on my lips, and my body hardened at the memory of her touch. "Sorry."

"For what? Telling it like it is? Don't be."

And just like that, she put me at ease. She asked me about school and my grades. She seemed so proud of me when I told her how well I was doing that I almost told her about my dreams; almost mentioned university and getting away from everything. But it was going so well, 'telling it like it really was' would have just spoiled it.

"What about a girlfriend? I bet you have girls throwing themselves at you."

I felt the heat as it scorched my cheeks and thanked the universe for the encompassing darkness.

"Not really." I'm not sure why I lied.

"I find that hard to believe." She cocked her head and raised an eyebrow. She looked almost comical in the dim glow of the street lights.

Batting away thoughts of sloppy kisses and soft breasts under the football stands, I cleared my throat and shifted in my seat. "Guess I haven't met the right one yet." I shrugged, thinking that would be that.

Instead, Rita stretched across the seats, and her hand settled just above my knee. I drew in a sharp breath. My eyes flickered to her face and back to the road. Ignoring my reaction, her hand remained where it was. In slow, delicate movements, her fingers traced a path up the length of my thigh and back again. A shiver of heat spread along my skin.

"Rita?"

She ignored me, letting her hands do the talking. She followed the same path up my thigh, but this time she didn't retrace her movements. Instead, she continued on to the waistband of my jeans where, with practiced fingers, she undid the button.

I swallowed the lump in my throat. "What the hell are you doing?" My heart pounded in my chest. It was all I could hear in the confines of the car.

She unzipped me and like a snake, her hand wrapped itself around my cock—which was already swollen and hard. I gasped. My left hand shot to her wrist, grabbing it but not pulling it away.

"Let go of my wrist and continue driving, Gabriel."

"Rita..." my voice was scratched and breathy. All the air had been sucked out of the car with the squeeze of her hand.

"Drive the car, Gabriel. Keep your eyes on the road and get us there safely. You wouldn't want me to have to tell uncle Tony what a naughty boy you are, do you?" She was pouting, but her eyes glinted with mischief.

"Rita... I..."

She squeezed her fingers just a fraction more. "Drive, Gabriel."

I did. It took all of my concentration and effort to remain seated, to keep my hips from grinding, from pushing my dick against her hand. My forehead was peppered with sweat, and my heart felt like it might burst.

My heavy breaths sounded rough in the car. Rita flicked on the radio; a popular song came on and she bobbed her head to the music, all the while squeezing and releasing me. Turning me on and off like a powerful engine. Go, wait, stop. Breath, squeeze, release. Tease, flick, pinch. Inhale, exhale—inhale, exhale.

Torture.

Pleasure.

Pain.

I was wrecked.

"Rita," I was breathing so heavily I could barely talk. "I can't do this much longer. Please let me go."

"Pull over."

"What?"

"There. Now!" I followed her gaze to the next street.

I turned onto a side street. Suburban, middle-class, bikes on green grass and perfectly manicured lawns; Subarus and Fords in driveways, curtains drawn and lights shining through gaps in white blinds; silence, except for my breathing. It was ragged and torn.

I was somewhere between agony and ecstasy, drowning

in need and burning with a fire I had not felt before. Jerking off was nothing like this.

I parked the car in the dark gap between street lights; the gap where darkness rules and monsters come out to play.

"Turn off the engine." Her voice was soft and velvety, inviting.

I did as I was told, her soft hand still on my cock.

"Push your seat back, Gabriel."

I bent over as her hand squeezed my shaft. I pushed the chair back as far as it would go and she released the pressure slightly. My stomach coiled with the sensation.

"Good." Our eyes locked, hers hooded and hungry. "Have you ever had anyone suck your cock, Gabriel?"

I nearly came at her words. I just shook my head, unable to speak.

Her sly smile grew and she bit her lower lip. I shut my eyes and sucked in breath.

"Help me." Rita tugged at my pants, suggesting I lift myself off the seat. I pushed myself up and helped her pull down my jeans and underwear. I pushed them down to my knees, where they remained like cumbersome chains. I was trapped in my own clothes.

She rearranged herself on her seat and licked her bottom lip, pulling it drawing in with her teeth, then leaned over.

My cock twitched as I felt her warm breath on the tip. Then her tongue swept over my head, and my heart smashed across my chest. My head fell back against the headrest, and my ass stuck to that leather seat, as my hips fought the sensation of pumping and thrusting.

Rita flicked her tongue over the tip, swirling it up and down my cock, eliciting gasps and groans out of me. I remember thinking that her tongue on my cock was the best sensation in the world. But, that thought only lasted a few seconds before she pulled me into her mouth with her next breath. I moaned as the hot, wet vacuum sealed around me and sent me reeling. Her hands cradled my balls, sending electric shocks of pleasure up my spine; my stomach wound and knotted; my thighs shook and quivered—and then, she swallowed me whole. Every inch of me disappeared down Rita's throat. The tension grew inside, and I could feel myself swell, grow, and pulse.

"Rita," I raked my hands through her hair, wanting to pull her off. "I'm going to come."

She pulled against me, increasing her pace, sucking harder. Like an electric bolt of pleasure, I found release in her mouth; a convulsing spasm as ecstasy washed over me. I groaned as my body jerked for a final time, and Rita drew every last drop from me, milking me till she was sated.

When I had settled, she withdrew and ran her thumb along her bottom lip.

I watched her face, in awe. I was spent and nervous and completely elated. Not even in my greatest imaginings, not once, did I think a woman could make me feel so different to the pleasure my hand did.

I reached over to pull my pants back up.

"Don't." She didn't shout it, but damn if she didn't command it. My ass fell back into the seat.

"Rita... I..."

"Start the car we need to get a move on."

I started the car, my limp dick exposed, my mouth spread in a goofy smile and heat searing my face. I wanted to cover up, to put myself away. But, like before, she surprised me. Her hand back on my shaft squeezing, releasing, taking, wanting, growing, swelling.

"Did you like that, Gabriel?" I nodded, my body a storm of emotions and sensations, none of which I had words for.

By the time we got to her Mustang, I was hard again. The pain and need back; the want of her mouth on me. Insatiable. I wanted her to take me again; I wanted those pink lips clamped around me.

My knuckles were white on the steering wheel when I finally pulled up next to her car. She had run it off the road. The passenger side kissed a tree and was dented, the metal twisted and angry. I felt a sudden pang when I saw that stunning body smashed up.

"We're here." She stated the obvious.

"Yup." I waited, knowing my fate was in her hand.

Literally.

"Turn the engine off."

I did as I was told. Honey-coloured light saturated the car from the dim street light up ahead. It lit up Rita's face and she smiled at me, her tongue trailing her top lip ever so slowly. I followed the movement with my eyes wanting that tongue on me, in me. I sucked in a long, desperate breath, and Rita released me. My cock stood to attention, awaiting its next command.

Rita grabbed the hem of her sweater and pulled it off, showing off her perky, beautiful breasts. Her pink nipples were hard and tight, and my fingers itched to touch her. Her skin cinnamon in the light. She reached back and undid the zip of her skirt. She pushed it down allowing the fabric to slide down her long, silky legs. My breath caught in my throat.

Her black G-string was all that was left. Rita jumped up and climbed between the seats landing in the middle of the back seat. Her legs spread open, her body somewhere between lying down and sitting up against the leather.

"Do you like what you see, Gabriel?" I swallowed hard. My throat raw and dry.

"Mmmm," it was a choked sound. My mouth a desert only Rita could quench.

Rita let out a soft moan and I almost lost myself. "Would you like to join me, Gabriel?"

I nodded but didn't move. Maybe I needed permission.

"Come here."

I fought against my pants, wanting to pull them up and down at the same time—wanting to be near her, on her, in her.

I wormed my way to the back seat and sat next to her, she moaned again and my cock jolted.

"Kiss me, Gabriel."

When my mouth tasted hers, my brain stopped working and my body took over. Thousands of years of instinct and mating unfolded inside me, like an ancient familiar map showing my body exactly what it needed to do. All of my fear, shame and hesitation fell away in an instant.

My mouth slammed into hers. It wasn't gentle or beautiful, but deep and bruising. Her wet tongue danced around mine in a mad battle. My body smothered hers as I pushed her down onto the seat. My hand found her naked breast, closing around it, cupping the hot flesh. My thumb flicked over a nipple, and she moaned into my mouth, sending my body into a frenzy. I swiped again at the hardening nub and Rita arched her back, pressing her breast into my hand. I was unravelling in her wonder.

My mouth unlatched from hers and kissed her neck, the scent of lilies, sweet and dizzying. I found her collar bone, settling kisses along her skin until I tasted that pink nipple—sweet and delicate flesh. I sucked and licked it, as she moaned and groaned, her body covered in a thin layer of perspiration.

My mouth devoured her, wanted her, and I let myself roam every inch of her torso. My fingers feeling where my mouth could not, playing a game of follow the leader.

She was magnificent. Exquisite really. Like watching a flower bloom or a volcano erupt. A natural phenomenon—violent, beautiful, vital.

I could smell the musk of her sex, an unfamiliar odour that fed my rigid hardness and fuelled my desire. My body ached for her. My erection painful, needing release, craving a warm, tight place.

"Slow down, Gabriel." she purred at me and pushed at my chest, lifting me from her.

"Take off your shirt." She lifted herself on an elbow and watched as I yanked my shirt from my body, eager and desperate. She let out a murmur of approval and a whisper of a smile flitted at her lips. "Not a boy anymore."

I pulled at my jeans; they had slid to my ankles, restricting my movement, caging me, driving me almost as insane as she was. I was fighting with the fabric when I stilled. My eyes glued to Rita's hands as they slid down to her G-string and in a single flexible movement, she lay naked before me.

I stared at the thin line of blonde hair that led to her wet lips. My mind reeled at the sight; my breath coming in short sharp gasps, anxiety and nervousness set in. I felt as if I had plummeted underwater and forget how to breathe. I knew where to find air, how to gasp at the surface, I just had to reach. I needed air to survive. My entire focus centred on this one singular thing—breathing, surviving—nothing else mattered, nothing else existed. That was her pussy to my sixteen-year-old self. Air. Without it, I was drowning. But then she moaned again and the adrenalin surged through my veins, masking all my uncertainties and unfolding the familiar map in my brain.

"Do you know how to put one of these on?" I have no idea where that condom came from, but she handed me the square foil packet.

I snatched the silver packet from her hand, my lungs straining for air. I fumbled with the rubber, rolling and tugging at the condom. The sensation, tight and strange, but it confirmed that I was about to lose my virginity to Rita Cancio.

She lay back onto the seat and invited me with a scorching a look, with her full lips and rounded hips.

My body blanketed hers and all I could feel was the warmth of her entrance as I rested there. "Are you ready?" My voice was tight, wavering.

"Yes." She smiled at me.

Rita lifted her hips to meet me as, ever so slowly, I buried myself in her.

Time.

Stood.

Still.

The squeeze of her pussy on my shaft mingled with her silky warmth, her mouth pouting in a near perfect 'o', letting the softest of moans escape. Her nipples hard against my chest, her blonde hair streaming down her back, the smell of musky lilies. It all etched itself into my memory. One I would relive in my mind in the months to come.

She started moving below me, my hips responding to her movements. I pulled out till just my tip was still inside then slipped back in, slamming against her. My arousal building—burning, scorching.

My hand shot to her breasts; I needed to hold her, suck her, fuck her.

She lit in me an unexplored hunger. I was a traveller discovering new worlds, and what a wondrous world Rita was. I revered her, and she rewarded me with soft moans. The car fogged over with our desire, perspiration covered the windows, and the leather grabbed onto my legs in a sweaty embrace.

Out of their own volition, my hips began to move, pounding against hers as she pushed herself against me, forcing me deeper. I wanted to sink right into her, wanted to fill all of her. I was crazed and frenzied as my body took on a life of its own. My hips grinding and pumping, the need for release like a burning fever.

I clutched her hips, trying to sink deeper, faster, harder. I pumped my hips furiously, her breasts bouncing, I licked her skin, needing all of her to be all over me.

Faster.

Harder.

Stronger.

Deeper.

Deeper.

Deeper.

And then I breached the surface.

I pushed her down as I jolted, clutching at her hips, sucking at her skin, and groaning a shuddering ecstatic release.

And just as I thought the miracle was done, She snaked her hand between us her; her fingers rubbing and stroking her clit as she pushed herself against me, forcing me deeper. I was awe as her insides convulsed and squeezed, milking my shuddering cock, sending shivers of delight right through my core.

I was spent and shattered and completely in awe.

I collapsed above her, her chest rising and falling, hot and sweaty against my own.

I never wanted to leave. I didn't want the feeling to end, the ecstasy to evaporate, or the warmth to diminish. But as we caught our breath, she pushed me gently on my chest, and I pulled away from her; my limp cock fell away from her warmth and rested in its plastic cocoon.

Rita kissed me on the cheek, her wild hair fell across her hardened nipples, her cheeks rosy and flushed. She looked beautiful.

I was in a post coital haze—drifting on the surface of the water, gazing at a starry sky, taking long, delighted gulps of air.

"Get dressed, Gabriel." Her voice pierced my daydream.

When I looked at her she was already mostly dressed, a finger tracing the outline of her mouth fixing her lipstick.

I reached for my shirt and pulled it on then tugged up my pants. She was already in the driver seat.

"Get out."

I opened the door, slid from the backseat and into the street. The electric window of the driver side came down in a soft whirr.

Rita reached out the window, a twinkling batch of keys hung off the ends of her fingers. I took the keys and she grabbed my hand, "That was sweet, Gabriel. I really enjoyed it."

"Rita…"

"It was fun, that's all. Now, you better not take too long, or uncle Tony will come looking for you." She snatched her hand away and winked at me. Her face broke into a smile, and she blew me a kiss. The car fell into gear and Rita raced off, leaving me rooted firmly back in reality.

I slumped into the front seat of the twisted Mustang and backed away from the tree. The metal sang and moaned as I peeled it away and turned back onto the road. I drove with the window down letting the cool night air sweep at my flushed brow and heated thoughts. Rita had taken me completely by surprise and, despite the delicate joy that strung itself around me, I also felt an immense sense of relief. My body sang and drowned in liquid ecstasy and confusion as the street lights whipped by and the radio crooned. And the world, for a moment, felt perfect.

Salvatore was waiting for me when I got back. We took inventory of the damaged car and made a list of the parts we'd need to order in the morning.

Before he left, he looked at me long and hard, as if considering saying something. Eventually, he settled on, "you better shower before Tony sees you in the morning."

I nodded, willing my face not to break into an adolescent smile. I clamped hard on my jaw and tipped my head. Salvatore left the workshop, and I went to the back room for my shower.

My body felt drained. Not tired, just empty—like I had run for miles. I stripped. I could smell evidence of Rita on my shirt, on my body.

I stepped into the steaming shower, the deluge washing away my sins. As I scrubbed away her smell, and the memory of her from my skin, my mind became clearer. I could reflect on what had happened in the back of that car.

The thing I learned that night was that, underneath her façade—underneath the makeup, and expensive clothes, and the perfume—Rita Cancio was just as dirty as me. My equal in humanity. She wasn't gold beneath a pile of coal; she was just a lump of coal flaked with gold dust that, when removed, was just as ordinary.

She was a great teacher but she would never be more than that. My mind flickered with guilt that was quickly put out by the water. The shower pelted at my back, and flashes of Rita played in my mind over and over like a movie. Those perky breasts and her sweet moans, the feel of her tight pussy squeezing around me. I was so hard. I stroked my shaft, pumping against my hand and spilling myself against the tiled wall. Rita may have taken my virginity but she didn't make me a man. That was going to come later.

I slunk to my bed tired and satisfied; and for the first time in months, I slept like a king.

—⁂

Popping my cherry only gave me an appetite for more. It wasn't love, not with any of them. It was a means to an end—an urge, a need. Momentary relief. If a line of girls wanted to get down on their knees and suck me off behind the bleachers, I wasn't going to stop them.

Sometimes I wish I wasn't so cold or so harsh with them. But they wanted more from me than just physical attention, and I wasn't ready to give it. And, in truth, none of those polished-up turds really deserved it. All their money bought was pretty, little mouths with red hot lipstick that sucked down on my cock.

I never thanked Rita. She wasn't looking for thanks. She came to pick up her car a week later. I was at school. I didn't even get to say goodbye. I may have felt a momentary pang about the whole thing. But Rita was just another shiny thing on a shelf full of shiny things, and my hands were too dirty to touch any of them. Life moved on.

I graduated top of my class—probably cause my head was clear. Nameless girls took care of my sexual frustrations, and I had no friends. The work at Tony's gave me hands on experience, so I grasped mathematical concepts and writing skills better than some.

Tony insisted that I invite Alice to graduation.

I refused.

And once again, he showed me that my life wasn't my own and choice was a privilege I was not privy to. The walls of my cage got a little smaller.

I wiped the sweat from my forehead as I walked down the park path. The park. I hated that place, probably because it was home for a while. But despite what you may think, the benches were never comfortable and the trees never offered any protection. At night the trees grew and distorted everything. They creaked and crept and didn't hide the sounds. I batted the thoughts away trying to silence the memories. The screams. The hurt.

I found her on the bench. Some time ago it became hers. It was just a known thing. I hated that fucking bench. But for whatever reason, I'm yet to burn it down.

Alice was sitting with some man who had his hand uncomfortably high up her skirt. If she was enjoying it, I'd never know. Her eyes were rolling around their sockets like lost marbles, and her mouth hung open.

"Get your fucking hands off her!" I didn't mean to roar; I didn't really care.

The man jumped up pulling his hand away. He scowled down at Alice. She bolted up at the same moment he stood up.

"Deal is off Alice," the man turned to walk away.

She jumped from the bench and ran after him, "No. No man, Derick, come back. Ignore this fucker, we can go somewhere else."

Derick snatched his hand from hers and stormed away. She stood for another few seconds calling his name.

When she turned back in my direction, her face was marred in a deep scowl. She stomped towards me on stick legs, her head seeming too big for her body which looked to have shrunk—again.

"What the fuck are you doing boy? You cost me a customer!"

"I'm not a boy."

She slowed down and stopped right in front of me. At eighteen, I loomed over her. She reached up; her bony hands brushed my skin. "You'll always be my boy." The creases softened around her eyes.

I jerked away from her hand. She let it drop and returned to her bench. She plummeted into the seat and patted her oversized denim jacket. She found a pack of smokes and fished it out.

"This is where you conduct business, Alice?"

"That's none of your concern." She pulled out her long, white cancer stick and shoved it in her mouth. She slid the lighter out of the box and flicked it. The flame danced around and she sucked in a long breath, the end of her cigarette burning orange.

The smoke blew from her mouth in perfect grey rings,

and she looked at me through them as if they were a looking glass that gave her focus.

"Well now you're here, kiddo, let me look at you." She patted the empty space next to her, and I fell down beside her.

She smelt noxious, like sour piss and rusted metal. She grabbed my jaw, her scrawny fingers digging into my flesh as she turned my head left then right.

"Looks like someone's been feeding ya." She let her hand drop. It wasn't an apology. Alice never apologised for being a neglectful parent. It was her way of asking me for her cut, because I owed her.

I pulled out a small parcel. The sauce leaked into the Glad wrap and coated the sandwich, which was sure to be soggy. Alice snatched it from me anyway. She scrapped the ember of her half-smoked cigarette on the sole of her shoe, pinched the end to ensure it was out, then tucked it behind her ear before unwrapping her soggy feast.

The sauce streaked down her chin and coated her cracked lips. She looked like a kid, a street kid—dirty and scared, vulnerable and unkempt. The thought didn't make me feel sorry for her, it just made me angry. This was my other future; the one I would be living now had Alice not sold me off to Tony. I know you still believe Tony took me in—gave me a chance, saw potential. But in truth, I was sold to the highest bidder. It would be years before I learned the cost and many more years after that wishing I didn't.

Alice slurped and swallowed her bite then looked at me, her eyes seeming clear and focused. "What do you want, kiddo? Why are you here?"

I took a long breath, maybe I was hoping to suck in some courage. "I'm graduating high school. Top of my class."

"Good for you, kid." She wrapped the sandwich again and stuffed it into her backpack. I hadn't noticed it till just then. It was as tattered and wasted as she was.

"You should come."

She laughed. More like cackled. My heart stung at the sound.

"Tony said I should invite you." At that, her laughter died and her hands twitched to her ear. Alice pulled at the cigarette stuffing it back into her mouth.

She lit it again. "I have nothing to wear."

"I'll get you something. You can pick it up at Tony's."

"Yeah, sure kid." She scratched at her arm—dry skin, black and blue. It was hard to know where the dirt began and the bruising ended.

"Hey, Alice?" She lifted her head to me, her eyes widened just a fraction, swollen with moisture. "Are you ok? Out here? Do you need anything?"

"How about a fifty, kiddo? Just to tide me over, you know? And maybe your momma can get a haircut or something for your special day?"

Of course, she was lying. Her free hand rubbed at her thigh; she needed a hit. I pulled out the money I prepared earlier. Her skeletal fingers snatched the fifty from my hands and, like a magician, she made it disappear.

I stood up. "Come by on Tuesday and pick up your dress. Graduation is on Friday. Can you remember that?"

"Of course I can. I'm not stupid, you know."

"What day is it today?"

"Don't worry, I'll be there Tuesday."

"Yeah. See you, Alice."

———

I cut through the park and a few side streets to get back to the shop. Bile coated my throat and I dry retched behind some dumpsters. I was angry again. I needed to punch something or someone. How much would that fucker Derick have paid her? How many times would she let someone do that to her before she got that fifty? My stomach convulsed and my hands curled into fists. All I wanted to do was break something.

I slammed through the red iron door and marched to Tony's office. Despite wanting to kick his fucking door down and use it to break his face, I knocked as gently as I could.

"Come." His porky breath called me.

When I stepped inside, he assessed me. "Is it done?"

"Yes." I hissed at him.

He just smiled and said, "Good. Now, sit down we have business."

We talked shop for over an hour. He unveiled his future plans, how I was an intricate and important part of that plan and how he had groomed me. The word made me want to retch; hot, sour bile boiled at the pit of my stomach. With each word that spilt from him, I could hear the gates of my prison slam shut, the bolts getting tighter the bars growing longer and stretching on forever.

A life sentence.

I nodded and agreed with everything he said, my mind too frazzled to really care. I eyed the half-eaten slice of black forest cake on his table. The plate peppered with brown crumbs and smeared with jam and cream. He had already eaten the cherries, the empty hole in the icing sat like a dimple on his porky face.

The slice could have fed three people and here he was, a singular human, shoving it all into his mouth. I thought of Alice and wondered how many meals she could make of that cake, I wondered how much meth that fifty would have bought her, and whether she would show up to pick up her dress or if the coroner would be picking it up for her.

When Tony finally let me go, I went down to my room. The anger had evaporated into the chair in his office, and all I had left in me was hatred; hatred for everything and everyone who had put me on this fucking earth, who had led me here, who had dangled a carrot in front of my face, only to take it away and feed it to the fucking Easter Bunny instead.

I laid on my bed and stared at the flaking ceiling, sucking in long calming breaths. I couldn't afford to be stupid; I had to bide my time. When you live on the streets long enough, you learn patience. Eventually, you either steal, find, or are given what you need. I had an abundance of patience. And I could wait. An opportunity would come and I would be free.

—⚹

The dress was a light blue; the light blue you think is the colour of icicles, but really it's the sky that's reflected in the ice. I bought the smallest size they had and knew it would still be too big, but at least it would bring out her eyes. It cost me two weeks salary, but my mom would look beautiful. Dead or alive.

I also bought her some soap and travel size shampoo, new underwear and a hairbrush. I left the parcel with Salvatore knowing, if she would come by, he was the best man to deliver the package—and probably the safest. He might ask for a blow job and give her an extra twenty. It was the best case scenario.

I have to admit that when I came back to the shop and saw the package gone, I was surprised. Maybe even a little relieved. I didn't expect her to come, let alone remember. But maybe she smelt the money all the way from the park.

It was all meant to be simple. All she had to do was look like she'd had a shower in the last two days, put on the dress, sit down, shut up and fuck off.

But alas, Alice fell down a fucking rabbit hole and she was pulling everyone down with her.

I woke up in a sweat, my shirt drenched and soggy, clinging to my body. It felt early, there was too much quietness in the world; but after the dream I had, I wasn't going back to sleep. The nerves had caught up with me.

I had somehow managed to survive that high school unscathed. Not only that, I had almost been popular. I could have been if I didn't have a leash around my neck. But the fringes suited me just fine, somewhere on the edge of the in and out crowd, something of a mystery. But I did survive and finished top of my class.

Even though my stomach was in knots, and I hadn't eaten since Wednesday, I have to admit I was just a little happy. Alice would actually come and see me do something great. It would almost make up for all the missed birthdays and parent-teacher interviews and nights on the street.

Almost.

The cold water helped. I splashed my face a few more times, washing away the night and the nerves. I took a quick shower and got dressed in my uniform. Tony had the blazer cleaned and pressed, it looked almost new. I combed my hair and brushed my teeth.

When I looked at the clock it was 6:03 am.

I sat on the edge of my bed and recited my speech. I knew it by heart but I still recited it, reading it off the cards, listening to the quiver in my voice and the thumping of my heart. I was already hating the day.

The shop came to life at 7 a.m. as it did every day. Salvatore walked in slamming that red door, announcing his arrival. The hum of the fluorescent lights oozed into my bedroom. I could smell his coffee. The strong double espresso drifted under my door. It was like groundhog day, except today I was planning on changing everything.

Thing is, plans rarely go to plan.

Salvatore greeted me with a giant smile and slapped me on the back. He wasn't a gentle man or a nice man, but he was still more present than most of the other men my mom brought into my life. Over the years we got to know each other, on the surface, neither of us was willing to delve deeper. Salvatore liked to talk, mostly about stuff that didn't really matter—like sports, the weather, the cars he liked and fights he saw. The best thing about random conversation? It makes you forget your worries, and you lose yourself in monotonous words. Salvatore was a time waster and a life saver. They went hand in hand, but only when he was talking. If he was quiet, then you knew you were in trouble and then he didn't waste time or save lives.

Tony showed up an hour later. He marched right up to me and shook my hand, almost like I was his equal. He had a brown mark just under his chin and a black seed stuck between his two front teeth.

"I'm proud of you, boy. Now, let's get this done so we can start the real work."

He didn't mince words or waste time. He ushered me toward the car that waited out front. The Lexus. I hadn't seen that car since the night with Rita. My legs wobbled as I climbed inside and slid across the back seat.

The car had that new car smell, even though he'd owned it for almost five years. Any evidence of Rita or I had long been polished off in the weekly clean. The car was waxed and shiny, much like its owner; except Tony was shiny from the amount of sweat he exuded.

Tony screamed down the phone at some poor fucker the entire time we drove. His cheeks turned beetroot pink, and I thought he might explode at any minute.

In fact, I was kind of hoping he would. When we pulled into the school, he pointed at the door. I left the car and walked in alone. It was almost poetic. I was finishing off in the same way I started—alone, with every eye in the room on me.

The hall was a hive of activity. Loud chatter. There were a lot of families, everyone else's families. I looked around hoping to catch Alice. When I didn't see her, I wasn't surprised. I took my seat and waited.

The crowd began to break apart and take their seats. Tony showed up as the principal took to the stage. His frown was deeper than the Southern Road Creek. His cheeks were crimson and sweat poured down his swollen face. He was huffing as he took his seat, and I knew that look in his eyes. He just wanted this over with so that he could go take care of his real problems.

I don't know why he stayed, maybe it was like signing a contract—he needed to see it to the end, make sure the T's were crossed and the I's dotted.

The principal blabbed on about something; I wasn't listening. I couldn't listen because I was looking, waiting. My stomach coiled and set in hard stone. Where the fuck was Alice?

When they called my name to speak, she still hadn't shown up. The empty seat beside me carried all my idle hopes, reminding me with every second of every other disappointment and let down. I took a long, galvanising breath and pushed it all down. Fuck her and her blue dress. This was all me, all about me and damned if she was going to take that away from me.

I started my speech. Something about standing on the shoulders of giants and tides lifting all boats. I stuffed that speech with so many clichés and metaphors that I wondered if anyone actually knew what I was talking about.

About halfway through my eloquent 'life is an ocean' metaphor, I heard the commotion in the back of the auditorium, but then so did everyone else; a few scrapped chairs, a thud and the distinct hoarse voice of the woman who pushed me out into the world.

"I'm here to see my kid." Her slur carried across the entire auditorium. My eyes flicked to Tony, whose face twisted in an ugly scowl. He nodded to Salvatore, who was leaning in the darkness against the wall. For a big man, he could move.

Alice had already forged a path through the spectators but, once she spotted Salvatore, she did a U-turn and pushed her way in the other direction.

A few hands reached for her, trying to stop her advance, but she was a scrappy one—always had been. She pushed them off wedging herself further into the auditorium, closer to the stage, closer to her seat.

I got a good look at her then. She wasn't wearing the dress; she was barely wearing anything at all. A ratty Micky Mouse top, that was cut like a halter, fell across her shoulder and showed off the straps of her black bra; a black skirt, that may have fit her once, barely clung to her protruding hips; worn black boots looked too big for her feet and that back-pack attached to her like it was part of her body.

My hands gripped the podium and my jaw clenched as she fought her way closer.

"Let go of me, you freaks! I just want to see the kid. He told me to come. Get your hands off me!" Her screams echoed in the large space. Suddenly, the limelight that shone above my head felt too bright and too hot. All the eyes on me were judging and mocking, full of pity and jest.

When Salvatore finally caught up to her, she was nearly in the front row. He grabbed her by the elbow and pulled on her. It might not have seemed like it to most, but he was being gentle. Very gentle. I made a mental note to thank him for that later. Or maybe not.

She kept fighting and didn't budge. Salvatore's hands closed against her bony arms, as he tightened his grip. I held my breath waiting for the snap. He tugged on her, as if she was nothing but a rag doll, and pulled her up so that her ear was level with his mouth. She stilled as he delivered what-ever message he had to say. Her eyes suddenly shrank in their sockets. I have seen that look before, but never on her;

it was fear. Her eyes flicked over to Tony who was glaring at her, his nostrils flaring and lips curling.

Alice shrivelled like a flower that has been standing under the sun too long. The fight seeped out of her and, with a simple nod, she allowed Salvatore to lead her out. Silence fell on the auditorium as all eyes fell onto my mother being led out like a stray dog. People returned to their seats and the heavy silence speared my heart.

Before Salvatore managed to get Alice to the door, her body jerked. She made a sound that could only be described as a cat coughing out a hairball as vomit erupted from her mouth in a brown, smelly projectile. It coated the wall. Small lumps of food hung onto the paint and dripped slowly onto the floor where the rest had pooled. Bile rose in my throat, and my heart smashed against my rib cage. I have never wanted her dead more than in that moment.

Judge me if you must.

The crowd erupted into nauseated wails, and the smell wafted over to the stage filling the hot space. I could swear I smelt deli meat. I wondered if it was the sandwich I had given her a week before.

Salvatore dragged her out and the door slammed with their exit. A heavy hand landed on my shoulder, and the principal's brown eyes were suddenly looking into mine. I knew the look, disgust mingled with pity. He pursed his lips and nudged me out of the way. I wasn't going to get to say my speech that day. He proposed a twenty-minute break to give the cleaning staff an opportunity to clean up. No one argued and the hall emptied out in record time.

I left the stage and resumed my seat in the empty auditorium. The silence felt less overwhelming now that it was empty and without the heaviness of eyes and judgement. I knew what awaited me outside.

The janitor walked in at some point, swearing and clearly unhappy, his cheeks were pink and his eyes slightly uneven.

They probably pulled him out of an early staff party, and he was already on number four or five, judging by his unstable gait.

Instead of wiping the vomit off, he seemed to be smearing it everywhere.

"Someone sure had a party, didn't they? Couldn't hold their shit together. Had to ruin my afternoon!" He mumbled to himself.

I stepped forward and he halted, realising he wasn't alone. I helped him out. "Yeah, some drunk mom that showed up."

He eyed me as if sizing me up then returned his attention to the wall. "Oh yeah? Heard she was a piece of work."

"Yeah?"

"Sure, sure. Someone said she looked like a prostitute. Maybe once I'm done here, I could catch her, maybe she can let me give her one up the ass for my troubles."

I sprang up from my chair so fast it fell backwards, the crack of the wood on floor echoing in the empty chamber. I marched over to him, my fists clenched. "Watch your fucking mouth."

I don't know why I didn't hit him, in the same way that I don't know why I was defending Alice. If he chased her, she would let him stick his dick up her ass; as long as he paid, he could put anything anywhere.

I towered over him as he wiped the floor. I let my fists fall to my side. "That's someone mother." His face pulled back and his lips swerved to the left in a look that said, "so?"

I pushed the nearest chair over as I crashed through the auditorium doors.

The hall was congested, bodies milling around. The murmur grew as they saw me. A few snickers and a few fingers flew about the room. Fuck them. I looked straight ahead. There's no way I am apologising for her behaviour.

I stepped outside, the hot morning air heavy and humid. I gulped in lungfuls of it. Suffocating.

I walked.

I needed to clear my head. I walked across the courtyard and past the oval, and soon I had left the school building behind. I suddenly knew I was never going to set foot in that place again. I didn't look back; I didn't need to. They would mail all the paperwork over, and that year would be the one remembered for not having a picture of the valedictorian in the yearbook. There would be no speech, but everyone would remember the vomit.

Fucking Alice, always the centre of attention but never the right kind.

My thoughts wandered to Tony. He would be embarrassed when I didn't show back up. He would sit there like an idiot for the next two hours without me. I wondered how long it would take him to realise that I wasn't coming back. My mouth cracked open for a split second. Fuck that fat fuck. Let him sit there and sweat. Let that big vein on his forehead throb—maybe it will explode. I knew I would be punished. I knew, that with the show my mom put on and the trouble he'd been having at the shop, Tony was under some serious stress. So I would probably get more than I deserved, but I didn't care. I was done being his prisoner, at least for the next few hours.

I let my legs carry me. I didn't know where I was going and it didn't matter. I found myself in the park. I sat on the bench, the same one I found Alice on earlier in the week. I tried not to think about it. Thoughts swirled in my head; anger and anguish mingled and crashed like waves, turbulent and angry like that ocean in the speech I never got to give.

I must have sat there for a long time because there she was. Alice—stumbling towards me. Her shirt was stained with her vomit, and the reek shot straight to my nose as she fell down beside me.

"What are you doing here, kiddo?" Her back was turned

to me, and she flipped her backpack off searching for a cigarette.

"Where is the dress, Alice?" I hissed through clenched teeth.

"What fucking dress?"

"The blue one? The one I bought you?"

"It was too nice and you chased off Derick…"

"Are you fucking kidding…"

I didn't finish the question because, as she turned around to face me, I saw her face—the split lip and swelling in her right eye.

"Alice…"

She sucked on her cigarette and blew out white smoke, "I'm sorry, kiddo. I really am. I tried to come, I tried to see you. But, you saw how they treated me." I could see the tears as they pooled in her eyes. "You looked so damn handsome standing up there." Her lip twitched.

"Is that all they did?" My fists clenched by my side.

"It's ok, kiddo, I've had worse."

"Let me take you to a shelter tonight."

"No."

"Alice."

She took another long drag from her cigarette. "I went all that way to listen to you speak. Why don't you tell me what you were going to say?" She leaned back against the bench and winced. I just stared at her. It wasn't the first time I had seen her beaten, but it had been a while. She looked so much more fragile, so much more breakable. Or maybe my heart wasn't strong enough, cold enough, hard enough yet.

"Stop staring and read me your fucking speech."

I clenched my jaw but, as always, I relented. I pulled out my cue cards, even though I didn't need them. I think I just needed something to look at other than her face. I got to say my speech that day in front of my mom. It wasn't the setting I was after, but it felt good. When I was done, I turned back to her. Her face was streaked with tears and I want to believe it was because of my words.

'The Hand' was not an uncommon name for men in Tony's line of work. They usually received the title for violent acts involving hands—like breaking hands or ripping them off, or using them to break your jaw or kneecaps. Not my Tony. No, he was called The Hand for his uncanny ability to force yours.

If that is unclear, let me explain.

Tony was a collector, not of things but of information. His mind was a vault and once a trickle of information managed to worm its way in there, it was in there forever. What Tony also knew is that without evidence or proof, much of his information was often useless So he had a real vault. Later, I would find it and all its contents and wish I never had. He kept evidence in it and, whether it was true or fabricated, that was Tony's weapon against everyone. He had an ability to find your weak spot and break you at the knees, without touching a hair on your head.

Today I was going to learn that lesson.

I gave my school blazer to Alice, knowing she would either use it or sell it for her next fix. Either way, I had no more use for the thing. By the time I got to the shop, the sun was setting and it bathed the streets in a beautiful orange glow.. I felt its warmth on my face as I crossed the street. I should have been more aware, but I was basking—maybe in the sun, or maybe in the tender moment with Alice—but I didn't notice that there wasn't anyone waiting outside the shop, even though Tony's car was still outside.

The smart thing would have been to turn and run, to get on a bus, or hitch a ride and vanish off the face of the planet. But I wasn't thinking, I wasn't even looking. I didn't see the monster at the end of the tunnel because I didn't realise I was walking into one.

I pushed through the big, heavy, red door and let it slam behind me as I always did. It was probably the lights that finally got my attention. The front house lights were switched off, while the back lights were on like beacons.

I froze. My heart leapt in my chest and I twisted around, my eyes scanning the darkness.

Salvatore walked out of the shadows. Of course they sent him, a friendly face to keep the mouse in the trap, to keep it calm. A shepherd leading the little sheep to its slaughter. My throat closed up, breathing became almost as hard as swallowing.

"He's been waiting for you for hours, Gabriel." He shook his head. "You know the boss doesn't like to be kept waiting." Salvatore walked towards me and hooked an arm around my sagging shoulders.

He stepped forwards forcing me to move. One foot at a time, I dragged my feet as my stomach rolled.

Two of Tony's men waited outside his office. They nodded at Salvatore and ignored me. Bile rose in my throat as I realised I was the walking dead.

One of the men reached for the door handle and opened it for us. Salvatore led us inside.

The two men shuffled inside and closed the door behind them. I was caged.

Tony sat at his desk. A new, clean suit adorned his wide shape, and his piggy face was as calm and collected as I had ever seen it. I was fucked.

"Good evening Gabriel, so good of you to join us at last." He cocked his head. "Do take a seat."

His eyes followed me as I shuffled to the chair across from his desk and fell like dead weight into it. I sucked in a deep breath and met his eyes.

"You missed your graduation." His jaw clenched beneath chubby cheeks

I remained silent.

"I don't like being made a fool of."

"I'm sorry Tony—"

"Be quiet now Gabriel, the adults are talking." He silenced me with his sharp tongue. "You know, you are an ungrateful little punk." Tony pushed against his chair, and it scraped the floor with a screech. He pulled off his jacket and placed it neatly on the back of the chair. He unbuttoned his cufflinks and rolled each sleeve in turn to just below the elbow, revealing pasty white arms covered in long dark hair.

He rounded the table, taking short measured steps. He came to a complete stop in front of me and, although I saw it coming, it caught me by surprise.

I saw his arm as it swung across his chest and then swung back around. The back of his hand connected perfectly square across my cheek and, without warning, he swung back smacking the other side of my face. The slap of skin on skin echoed against the walls.

My cheeks stung at first then heat rose like wildfire, getting hotter and hotter as it burned across my face. I could feel tears well in my eyes, but I pushed them back and straightened my spine. Tony smirked as I held his gaze.

"Hold him."

Three pairs of hands yanked me from the chair and threw me across the table. Panic gripped me.

"No." I fought and thrashed against the men. I would not allow this again, the humiliation of it. But I was outnumbered and out powered.

My heart smashed against my ribcage as I fought.

"I said hold him!"

The three men tightened their grips and pulled on my limbs. A heavy weight fell across my torso, and I was glued to the table. A hand pushed my head down, my cheek grinding against the polished wood.

Hands moved around my waist, fiddling with the button of my pants.

"No! No! Tony…" I was begging even as my ass felt the cool of air of the air conditioner.

I flinched at the first crack. Memories flooding my brain. I clenched my teeth and sucked in the heavy air. I wasn't going to give him the satisfaction of crying. Tony's belt connected with my skin over and over again. The deluge of pain felt endless until the searing fire grew warm and leaked across my back. The men had fallen silent and still, the belt licked and bit and punished. My body would not endure much more. I could feel my senses fading.

"You!

Will!

Never!

Walk!

Out!

On!

Me!

Again!

Do you understand?" Which each word the belt cracked like thunder, harsh and brutal.

I tried to nod but the hand on my head pushed against me.

"Yes, Tony." It came out like a whisper, weak and pathetic. I thought I was a man, until I was shown that I wasn't. That would come later.

"Good." He threw his belt on the table an inch from my face and returned to his seat, falling into it heaving.

The hand on my head pulled and twisted until I could see Tony.

Crossing his hands across his mountainous belly, he looked at me in that way of his, a way I have seen him looking at others—like a predator that knows he has you cornered, though you don't know it yet. Except, I knew it.

I could feel the blood as it oozed off my back and pooled on the table, the very air burning my wounds. I have never felt so vulnerable.

"Now that that's out of the way, let's talk business, shall we?" He had a smug smile on his face and I gritted my teeth. Resistance was futile.

"Now that you are a graduate with a fucking diploma, I think it's time for you to make some investments." His hands tightened around himself. "I mean a boy like you, with nothing, can finally make something of himself. I'm sure you'd hate to end up like your mother." His smile stretched and I flinched at the mention of her.

"Leave Alice out of this." I hissed.

"But why? A boy like you, neglected, unloved? I can take care of her for you, bring her over, have the guys give her a once over. Maybe put her to rest once and for all."

He was watching me. He needed my reaction and like a fool, I gave it to him. I wasn't ready to go against him yet.

My knuckles turned white as I clenched my hands into tight fists. My locked jaw ached and I could feel the rage, the hatred, and the anger bubbling.

Now, I may have been angry but I wasn't stupid. I was still naked and bleeding on his table.

"That won't be necessary. Thank you, Tony." That was all he needed. My surrender. I had just given him all he needed to hold me by my leash.

"If you're sure?"

"I'm sure." I sealed my fate.

Alice or me. Fuck Alice. Here she was getting me in to more trouble. I wished I could hate her more, I wish I'd wanted her dead but fuck it, she was my mom after all.

Tony nodded, reached over, and pulled a wad of paper

from his top drawer. "I have a graduation present for you, Gabriel."

He placed the wad of papers on his desk, right in front of my face.

"What is it?" My breath was coming in short heavy pants. The pain in my back and legs intensifying, scorching, flaying my skin. I needed to close my eyes. My senses grew dimmer.

"It's your new car wash."

I remained silent. What the fuck was he talking about?

I waited.

When he saw I wasn't going to speak, he finally explained. "The pizza place, the hotel, and this here shop are doing well —very well, in fact, too well. We can't keep up with the laundry and so we need a new outlet. Lucky for you, you are now the new owner of the car wash down on Fifth."

My jaw clenched tighter, and I swear I could feel my teeth sink deeper into the gums.

"You, as the new owner, will operate my new business." He cleared his throat and smiled, "*Your* new business. However, you will report to me weekly with both sets of books."

I took a few deep breaths. My head was throbbing, the hand forcing it down pushed harder, and my body felt like it was starting to shut down. "What if I refuse?"

Tony's face broke into a smirk and he huffed. He uncrossed his arms and bent over so that his mouth was by my ear. The heat of his breath was saturated with ham. "Salvatore here will call the boys, and Alice will join us within the hour. I will make sure she suffers, and I will make sure you get to watch. You can watch her swallow every dick I feed her, then you can watch as I make her choke on it."

I could feel powder in my mouth as my teeth ground together.

"Now, now son; we all know that if she chokes on a dick, she'd have eaten something before she died."

He burst into hysterical laughter, and I could hear Salvatore's cackle from behind me.

I kept breathing. All I had to do was move, and I'd be the one swallowing dicks.

"Where would you like me to sign?" My voice was scratched and hoarse.

"That's a good boy now."

Someone shoved a pen into my hand and, one by one, Tony flipped papers in front of my face. I scribbled my name as the pen hung loosely from my hand. I must have signed thirty different contracts; I didn't need to read them to know what they would say.

The thing about having a boss like Tony is that he acquires all the wealth without doing any of the work. His name didn't show up anywhere, although he was everywhere, and his hands were in a hundred different pies. The man was a fucking ghost.

He owned a mid-sized house in the suburbs, and his cars were all legally purchased. Well, the ones his wife and daughters drove around. There was no trace of him anywhere in any of his businesses; and that's how he got away with it all. Pin the tail on some poor schmuck and pretend you know nothing. Today, I was said schmuck.

When I'd signed the last contract, Tony took the papers away and shoved them back into the drawer.

"Good boy." He patted me on the head. I wanted to kill him. "Let him go. Salvatore, take him downstairs and have him cleaned up."

The pressure on my head and torso disappeared. My limbs were released and suddenly I felt weightless. I pushed against the table, standing up. I winced as my body protested, my muscles burning, my skin hanging on by a thread. I flinched when I felt a hand on my shoulder. Salvatore was by my side.

He held me up as I pulled up my pants and left my dignity

in shreds on the office floor. Salvatore helped me downstairs and to my room. I yanked my hand from his grip and slammed my door in his face—a small victory in the very large battle I had just lost.

"Hey," Salvatore's deep voice came from the other side of the door, "let me help you clean up."

"Why don't you fuck right off?!"

He didn't answer. I knew he was going to be outside my door all night and, that somewhere in the park, a few of Tony's men had eyes on Alice. Hell, they probably had their hands on her, too. I wondered if she liked it. Didn't really matter, not as long as she was going to get paid.

I threw my limp shirt against the wall and let my pants and underwear fall to the floor. Each movement elicited a wince. The pain refused to remain in one spot; it wasn't sharp, but rather I felt as if I had been held under boiling water. My skin felt singed and scolded and, with each movement, the pain spread across my back in waves.

I staggered to the bathroom, a trail of red blood staining the floor.

I caught a glimpse of myself in the mirror, my complexion ashen and sweaty. My stomach lurched, nauseated. I stepped into the shower and turned on the cold water. My body convulsed as water beads fell against my skin. I sank to my knees, the red water swirling around my hands. Bitterness crawled beneath my skin and gripped my insides.

A path had been carved for me whether I liked it or not; my life has been decided by a sandwich eating motherfucker, and I had no say. I was in the world's biggest prison—my own life—and there was nothing I could do about it.

I staggered from the shower; the searing pain eased to a throbbing, aching reminder that played havoc with my brain. My mind conceded to the torment and began to shut down. I fell onto my bed, and everything went black.

It took a week to set up the car wash. Salvatore didn't

leave my side. Apparently, he came with the business; a package deal of sorts, except that he had no benefits. He was just my shadow, like another reminder of all the looming darkness if I was to set a foot wrong.

At the end of the week, I cleared out my room in the shop and moved into the upstairs apartment of the car wash. I hated it. I couldn't sleep. It was too quiet and it smelt way too good, all soapy and flowery where I was used to smelling oil, lubricant, sweaty men, and exhaust pipes. I felt eight all over again, homeless and alone.

For the next six months, I did nothing but work. I trained staff and watched them clean cars while I cleaned money. Once a week, I would go into Tony's office and every hair on my body would stand to attention. The welts he had left on my back would spring up and the feel of the air conditioner on my face brought bile to my throat. Tony felt my discomfort. He had set it in there, let it harden, and tormented me with it. Our meetings extended longer than they should and, like a sadistic fuck, he would watch me flinch and sweat and squirm.

What Tony didn't know is that although he asked me to keep two sets of books, I kept three. Salvatore was too stupid to notice, and Tony was too busy playing mind games. He probably thought I was too afraid or too broken to ever steal from him; but, fuck it, I had plans.

But like most things in life, even the best-laid plans never really go the way we hope.

PART III

My breath hung in the air in a wispy cloud. Even under the blanket, I felt the chill as it settled around the room. It seeped through the floor. That place was perpetually cold. I often wondered if it was the design of the building. I mean, it was basically one giant wind tunnel. Other times I thought maybe it was because I always saw it as my tomb. Tony knew how to dole out punishment.

Hair stood on the back of my neck when bottles clinked somewhere outside. The noise pierced the darkness like soft bells. It was an odd sound at 3 am. There shouldn't be anyone around. I grabbed the bat I kept under the bed and tiptoed down the stairs. My stomach rolled and my heart thumped in my chest as I heard the shuffling. It was coming from the back of the building; someone was trying to break in.

My fingers curled around the doorknob, I could hear the bottles tinkling again. I yanked the door open, a gust of cold air pushed against my face. My hand squeezed the bat, coiled and ready to swing at whoever was digging through my trash.

The tail took me by surprise.

The animal's head shot up, scared eyes glimpsed into

mine, then it took off like a bullet. It slunk behind the dumpster, keeping to the shadows. I held on to the bat, my fingers tightening around the wood. As I rounded the dumpster, I expected bared teeth and claws. Instead, it was cowering behind a scrunched-up, plastic sheet trying to make itself smaller. My grip on the bat loosened.

"Hey there buddy, you lost?" The dog took a shaky step backwards, his nails clicking on the bitumen. "Come here, I won't hurt you."

As if he understood, the dog lifted his head. His brown fur shone yellow under the dim backdoor light.

"You lost? You hungry?"

The dog remained where it was.

I took a tentative step forward, and the animal pushed himself into the wall, his tail tucked between his legs, a low whimper fell from him—a pitiful whining sound.

"Wait here." I eased backwards, taking slow measured steps until I was at a safe distance, turned back to the door and stepped inside. I took the stairs two at a time and flung my fridge open, scanning the contents.

Dogs liked milk, didn't they?

The bottle was mostly empty, and the milk sloshed around as I ran downstairs. I found an old bowl near the pantry and tucked it under my arm as I stepped outside again. I rounded the dumpster, my chest heaving.

The dog was gone.

I scanned the street, squinting in the dark looking for a hidden shadow. I saw nothing. My numb hands fell to my side. I sighed, my breath coming out in a long plume of white. I turned towards the door and had one foot inside when I heard the whimper.

I swung back around. The dog was about twenty paces away sheltered in the shadow of the neighbouring building. His scared eyes reflected like yellow pools in the street light.

I put the bowl down and filled it with milk. "Come here, boy."

I whistled softly.

The dog kept staring at me, he paced a little, not coming any closer. I called him a few more times. When he didn't budge, I left the milk and walked back inside. I closed the door and leaned against it, peering through the small window.

The dog waited. He probably smelt me, but I had no intention on venturing outside again. I ignored the biting cold as it stung my skin and clawed at my bare legs. My eyes stayed glued on the animal.

The dog edged out of its hiding place. His nose sniffing constantly, his eyes looking around, shifting and scanning. Now that his face was in the light, I could make out the long snout and shaggy hair.

He skirted closer to the bowl, rounded it a number of times and, with a final sniff of the air, began to lick the milk. He was nearly done when my foot scuffed the door. His head shot up, and his eyes met mine for a split second. Before I could react at all, he bolted into the darkness.

I waited, staring at the black street, knowing he wouldn't be back. Eventually, when I could no longer contain the chattering of my teeth, I went back to bed. I couldn't fall asleep. That fucking dog reminded me of Alice. I hadn't seen her in almost six months and the last two have been cold. Frigid. I tossed and turned until the friction of my body against the sheets warmed me enough to pass out into a fitful sleep.

The dog came back every night that week. For the first two nights, I saturated bread in milk; by the third day, I bought some dog food; on the fifth night, he stood waiting, not in the shadows and not by my door, but close enough that I could make out its face. At first, I thought he was a Border Collie—he had the light underbelly and long snout— but as he got closer, I realised he was an Australian Shepard.

His long coat was dirty and sticky in parts, the fur clung together in clumps. His ears were matted, and he had two perfectly round bald spots by his left ear, as if someone had used a cylinder of some kind to hurt him, mark him, brand him. He was young, not a puppy but not quite an adult— hanging somewhere on the fringes.

By the sixth day, he allowed me to sit on the stairs and watch him eat. He gulped the food, and the street echoed with crunching. Each time I moved, he would freeze and eye me. His body tense, his legs doubled up, ready to bolt. I admired him from afar; this desolate miserable runt, unloved and broken, needing shelter and food. It was like looking in a mirror.

When the dog finished his meal, he sat down next to the empty bowl. We watched each other for a while and, deep in his watery eyes, I thought I saw recognition. I wonder if he saw me for what I really was.

"Come here Spots. Come here, boy." I patted my thighs and waited. The dog cocked his head then took off into the darkness.

Progress.

Work was shit, an endless line of cars that needed to be cleaned.

My life was spent watching others polish and wax shells. But, what I craved was to see the heart and valves of the machines, to smell the oil and petrol and let it coat my hands. I needed to bend and twist wire, screw bolts and replace washers. I missed the shop. I missed working with my hands. My cramped office stank of flowery soaps and chemicals.

Money kept rolling in and out, and the books had to be kept in order. Three sets of books; one for the tax man, one for Tony, and a third that only existed in my head. Turns out, placing numbers in columns and making other numbers disappear or reappear in another column came quite naturally to me.

I started saving. I know you might use another term, like skimming off the top or outright stealing, but I liked to think of it as a retirement fund. One on which I could actually retire, a sum that would help me disappear—just like the bills did.

Salvatore knocked on my door at 10 am sharp every Tuesday. "You ready to go, boss?"

"Sure, let me grab my coat." I stood up and peeled my jacket from the back of the chair. "And, I've told you to stop calling me that."

It was a short drive. If it was up to me, we would have walked. But things were never up to me. We pulled up outside the shop, and I looked at it with longing. Despite what I had been telling myself over the last year, trying to convince myself the car wash was my new home, I still felt like a stranger there. I couldn't settle. The shop was my home. It was where I belonged.

I pushed open the red iron door, letting Salvatore catch it in my wake.

The shop floor was full of cars, each in various stages of repair; some with their engines exposed, others with their wheels off. My fingers itched to get in there. I was eyeing a Mercedes; its engine sat exposed and the cylinder head removed. I took a step closer. I wanted to see the problem, solve the problem—even if it was with my head and not my hands. I stuffed my hands deep into my pockets, and that's when I walked into something covered with a plastic sheet.

I stopped dead and studied the object rubbing against my hip. I grabbed the corner of the plastic and peered beneath.

My heart stopped.

A Harley Fatboy sat broken beneath the sheet. I can't actually call it a motorcycle, all that was left was a burned out frame. The seat was still attached but was scorched and scared; the wheels were gone and headlight blown out. A single footrest hung limply from the right-hand side. I was smitten.

My heart thumped in my chest. I was in love. I needed that bike like I needed to breathe.

Salvatore walked up behind me and cleared his throat. I pulled the plastic sheet back over the bike, almost reverently, and led the way to Tony's office.

"Good morning, Tony." I hissed.

"Do you have what's mine?" He didn't need pleasantries. In fact, since I left him at my graduation, he had been icy cold.

"Here you go." I handed over the books and he skimmed them.

As always, this was more of a show than a necessity. He was showing me that I was a dog and he was my master. He could pull the leash at any time and I would sit, roll or play dead. We both knew it; he just thought I needed constant reminding.

Each time he skimmed the books and didn't find the leak I created, I grated my teeth and forced my self-satisfied smile to remain buried. Tony was smart, he should have seen it. But he was looking for a missing bucket of water, when all I was siphoning were tiny drops.

I guess as long as he saw money in his basement and the walls of his home, in the walls of the pizza shop and under the car wash, he didn't care.

His stubby fingers traced the lines of numbers. He stood up and his chubby fingers patted my cheek, "Good boy." He smirked.

Condescending fuck.

"You can go now; I have a busy day." He waved his hand in dismissal and fell back into his chair.

"Tony?"

His eyes rolled up at me, dissatisfaction ploughed his brow, a thick vein ticked on his forehead. In the silence, Salvatore took a minute step back—a micro movement. Tony lifted his head in full when he realised his scathing look wasn't going to get rid of me.

"Whose Harley is on the shop floor?"

"What business is that of yours? You have your own business to look after."

"And I do. Very well." I straightened my shoulder and sucked in every inch of bravery I had left. "I would like to fix it, please."

"Fix what?"

"The Harley."

"That burned out piece of shit?" He cocked his head, the creases on his brow deepening.

"Yes."

Tony's astute gaze bored through me. He snorted and his body shifted towards his desk. "I'm not paying for any parts."

"Of course."

"And it best be after work hours. I don't need you in my way, or the car wash losing business because you're distracted."

"Of course."

"I don't need you to agree with me." His hands fell flat on his desk as his head snapped back in my direction.

"Yes, Tony."

"Now fuck off, you're putting me behind."

I felt almost weightless as I took the steps one at a time. I stuffed my hands in my pockets, pinching my skin, forcing my face to remain taut and expressionless. Although my hands itched to glide over the ruined body of the bike, I had to go back to work. I walked out without a second glance at the covered bike. Tony made it clear that pissing him off would only bury me in more shit. I didn't want to give him an inch.

For the first time since I started at the car wash, the day didn't feel like it was at a standstill. I stared at the books and inhaled the noxious fumes of overindulgent perfume, but my mind was focused on head gaskets and transmissions, crankshafts and frame bolts. That day I built that bike in my head ten times over. I saw with perfect clarity what she might look like when I was done with her.

It was agony to wait, but I would. I couldn't be too eager. I also couldn't afford any parts, not with my meagre salary. Paying for parts with my stolen money would raise more suspicion than I cared to attract. Once again, Tony gave me an impossible gift and he knew it.

The staff cleaned up and cleared out. I locked up, went upstairs and got in the shower. The hot water pelted my skin, searing it. My body ached with the need to make, to fix and mend. I needed that bike, it was all I could think of. I don't know why I was so obsessed. Maybe it was because I saw another broken thing that I thought I could fix; the need to take something so mangled, so wrecked and turn it into something beautiful. Maybe if I could fix that bike and fix that dog— maybe, just maybe—I could also fix myself.

I pulled on my long slacks and hoodie, and` grabbed a beer from the fridge. The cool liquid sizzled against my hot throat.

I sank the plastic bowl into the bag of dog food and went downstairs to start my vigil. The freezing concrete floor burned through my clothes. I placed the bowl at my feet. Then I waited.

A whimper cut through the silence and my head jerked to the right, my hand knocking over the empty beer bottle. He was standing in the middle of the street, eyeing the food by my feet, but he didn't approach. Even after all this time, he didn't trust me. Maybe he could smell what really lay under the surface. I can't say I blame him.

"If you want to eat, you're just going to have to come here

and trust me." I wasn't trying to be soothing or quiet, it was all so matter of fact. Life sucks; it throws you around and beats you up, but you have to get up and keep going. You can't hide in the shadows.

The way I saw it, I gave this dog all the time it was going to get. If it wanted to eat, it would have to give me something in return. It might sound cruel to you, but his companion-ship was something I needed just as much as he needed mine.

We both waited.

Spots scampered a few steps forward and whimpered. I just looked at him. I didn't make any move to stand or walk or breathe. I just wanted him to come over so I could get a good look at him.

When he was five steps away, I could hear his stomach growling. Or maybe that was just him. I was forcing him, I was making him uncomfortable but, fuck it, nothing ever happens if we always stay in our comfort zone. We don't grow or evolve, and this fucking dog was going to love me whether it wanted to or not.

His dance of uncertainty continued. The tension of the standoff eased out into the world as Spots took the final few steps to the food bowl, relenting at last. I didn't move as he chewed his food; the crack of the biscuits sounded like breaking bones, saliva coated his lips as he gulped and sucked. He kept his eyes firmly on me, his right leg rigid in readiness to flee.

Now that he was close, I could see how damaged he really was. Those two scarred spots on his head were not his only marks. Someone really went to town on this guy. No wonder he didn't want to trust me. I didn't move until he finished eating and backed away.

When he was at a far enough distance, I grabbed the bowl and stood up. He didn't bolt. "That wasn't too bad now, was it?"

When I pushed the door open, he turned away and scuttled back into the shadows. I felt like I had finally gotten through to him.

By the end of that week, I moved the bowl to my side. Spots took less time to come near me, but being so close made him edgy. I could see it in the tightness of his mouth, in the tension of his legs and the way his tail was stiff and still.

I pretended that I didn't care. I let him eat and watched him go. Still, it was progress.

PART IV

I waited three weeks before I let myself think about that bike, and another two before I decided it was safe enough to go and have a good look at its wreckage.

I wonder if it was because I kept looking at the clock in his office that Tony dragged out yet another unnecessary meeting. I hardly paid attention to anything he said, my mind firmly fixed on the body waiting for me downstairs.

When Tony had grown bored with torturing me, he dismissed me unceremoniously with his usual, "Now fuck off."

I obliged. I took the stairs one at a time fighting tight muscles that ached to leap to the bottom. I ground my teeth, willing my expression to remain stoic. I stuffed my hands into my pockets and, in my efforts to seem causal, walked too slowly and too deliberately. If I was trying to avoid attention my gait did just the opposite.

Salvatore smirked and shook his head.

I stared at the hump beyond the sheet for a second before I tore it away and exposed the bike's naked frame.

I sucked in a long breath at the sight of it. The damage was worse than I had first thought.

The frame was scraped and burned, but still intact. There was no obvious crash or crack damage. Some of the tension left my body with the discovery. It would still need to be sandblasted and coated, if I was going to rebuild on it.

I would need an engine. I toyed with the idea of a 107 cubic engine, but that would depend on my funds. I already envisioned the ripple exhaust pipe and the ape handlebars. My fingers traced the stitching of the ruined gunfighter seat that would need replacing, too.

I made a mental list of the parts I would need. My mind churned at the possibilities. It would take a few months to get the body cleaned and coated. I could use that time to collect the parts I needed. I knew Tony had some bits and pieces in the back. I could create an inventory, set a budget and I would know how much I would need to steal, so I can pay Tony with his own money.

My mouth split open at the idea.

I grabbed the sheet and tucked the frame away. I would be back that night to sift through his stock. Excitement coursed through my veins. I sucked in a deep breath, hiding any sign of pleasure and met Salvatore by the door.

The moment I made the decision to return to the stock room that night the clock stopped moving and the day dragged on, despite a deluge of stupid customers and equipment breakdown. As the day wound down, coming to a close, I had the displeasure of a confrontational, irate woman who insisted that we scratched her car. On closer examination, the alleged 'scratch' was evidently a large, twisted dent in the back. After a short probe, she admitted that she reversed it earlier that day and thought her husband would be less likely to be angry if she explained that it happened at the car wash. I wished her luck and gave her a sympathetic car freshener. Then I welcomed her to fuck right off.

I didn't bother with a shower. I knew I was just going to get dirty again in that dusty, dark storeroom. I pulled on my torn-up work jeans. They were stained with oil and grease, but they were comfortable and homely. I pulled on a black t-shirt and my hoodie. I sucked down a beer, waiting for the sun to disappear and the world to turn black. I stuffed down a microwave dinner, and I waited.

Spots arrived just before midnight. With some hesitation, he walked right up to me and ate. I waited for the slurping and chomping noises to fade away. We watched each other for a second, and I stood up. Spots sank backwards towards the wall, cowering in fear.

"Hey buddy, I'm not going to hurt you. I just have to go. I'll see you tomorrow." With as much care as I could muster, I squatted down once more extending my hand. I held it up, my palm open. The muscles in my legs began to cramp, and my arm grew tired. I was about to retreat when Spots stood up and sniffed, then buried his nose against my hand for a second and proceeded to lick. My heart wedged itself in my throat, and I thought it might burst.

And then, as if he knew how much I needed it, he wagged his fucking tail. My eyes filled with tears that I brushed away. I stroked his head, feeling the rough scar tissue for the first time. The unevenness of lumps and bumps beneath his matted fur grated against my fingers.

"It's ok buddy, I'll look after you now. No one will ever hurt you again." He panted and wagged. Fighting screaming muscles, I stood to my full height, and he cowered again whimpering.

"Don't do that buddy. I won't hurt you." I held my hand out again and let him relax. I patted his head and stroked the length of his body.

"Ok I have to go; I have a hot date." I winked at the dog who cocked his head. I stepped off the curb and crossed the street. I could hear the scratch of nails on bitumen behind me. Spots was following keeping his distance. I kept walking, throwing occasional backward glances. Spots followed.

"You don't have to be so far away, buddy. Just come here."

He didn't.

I shrugged and made my way to Tony's.

I unlocked the heavy iron door and pushed through it. "Are you coming?" Spots waited across the street; I could just make out his eyes as they reflected in the street light. He didn't budge. "Suit yourself."

I closed the door gently expecting stark darkness, which is why the illuminating lights from Tony's office took me by surprise.

A chill ran down my spine. Tony was a resourceful man. He held information over other people's heads and, for all intents and purposes, he kept his hands clean, leaving the dirty work for others. Shit just slid off him, as if he was coated in Vaseline. So, to find him in his office in the early hours of the morning could only lead me to a handful of possible conclusions.

I grabbed a wrench, the weight comforting in my hands and glued myself to the wall. I slid along the wall, my shirt catching on the uneven plaster. My mind ran through the possibilities.

One. Tony had his dick deep in some woman. That would be the ideal situation. I would apologise and slink away, and my code of silence would remain intact as it always had. Bitter disgust unfurled itself in the pit of my stomach.

Two. Maybe it wasn't even Tony; maybe it was some punk who broke in. Maybe if I caught this thief and serve him up to Tony, all would be forgiven and Tony would bring me back from the exile of the car wash. My fist tightened around the wrench.

I listened, straining my ears. Silence. No shouting or talking or moaning. No ruffling of papers or opening drawers. My first two theories were starting to crumble, which left me with just one more. One which sent my heart into a gallop, and the hair on my skin prickle.

Tony was in trouble, and I just stumbled into whatever he was hiding. He would have heard me calling for Spots. I was a dead man.

I crept up the stairs, the lights from the windows casting long, yellow squares across the shop walls. The office door was open just a crack and I wound my fingers around the aluminium knob.

"Come in." At the sound of his steady voice, my heart somersaulted in my throat and landed with a thud at the pit of my stomach.

I took a galvanising breath, tucked the wrench behind my back and pushed the door open.

Tony leaned back in his chair facing the door, his arms crossed over his bulging stomach. My eyes flickered over his desk—books, photos and paperwork were spread across it.

"What the fuck are you doing here?"

"I came to work on my bike. You said after hours..."

He nodded, brushed his hands over his face and studied me. I could feel the chill as it descended around me; whatever I had walked in on was not something Tony would allow me to share. I had stumbled into quicksand, and I was suddenly sinking. Whatever this was, I needed to find a way out and disappear. Tony would have called someone as soon as he heard me. People would be on their way. My life was about to come to an abrupt end.

"Seems like you have come in at an inopportune moment." He sniffed.

"I could come back another night..."

"No, stay, why not put that brain of yours to work?"

We both knew he was buying time. In a few minutes, the red iron door would burst open, a group of men would spill inside, and I would never be seen again. I wondered for a second if Spots would miss me.

Tony reached for the sandwich he had on the edge of the desk, I could see the mayonnaise as it oozed over layers of deli meat and lettuce. The crunch of the lettuce cut through the icy silence between us as he bit off a big chunk and began chewing. A glob of mayonnaise pasted along his lips.

At first, he coughed. His face twisted into a scowl, and he coughed again. His eyes shot to me, and his pudgy hands reached to his throat. His coughing became forced, longer and agitated. His eyes grew wider and slowly crawled out of their sockets. I watched as he flailed, pleading with his eyes, clawing at his throat, as drool and snot gushed from his flaring nostrils.

I stepped back as he reached towards me, his forehead breaking out in a sweat, his face turning a shade rosy.

Burning crimson.

Saturated scarlet.

Swelling with effort.

The pleading in his piggy eyes burnt with anger for a fleeting moment and then turned to desperation. His body shook like a blob of jelly on his chair as he fought for air, whizzing and gurgling. I could see the disbelief on his features as he gasped in slow, shallow breaths that didn't reach his lungs. His hands fell by his side.

Tony was a powerful man, both in physique and within the empire he had built himself. To die by choking was as ironic as it was pathetic. This was not the death he deserved, but it was the death I was going to give him.

It was him or me, and we both knew it. I wonder if he found solace in not dying alone. I wonder if that's what all murders ask themselves.

He suffered. I knew he did. His body twitched, and his fingers jerked and jolted as he fought and tried to suck in air.

Tony chortled and whizzed and took his last breath, sagging like limp bacon onto his chair. The ruddiness of his ruby stained face faded; his lips tinged with blue. He stared at me through dead, bloodshot eyes. My heart slammed against my chest as if it was trying to beat enough for two people. I knew I didn't have long, but I waited—made sure.

When I was certain he was gone, I sucked in stale air and crept around him. I scanned the documents on the table. The pictures were the worst. They will be burned into my memory for the rest of time. I collected them anyway, stuffing them inside a book that held dates and names. That was the jackpot, the coveted treasure; everything else was just a bonus.

Or a curse.

With a quick scan of the other books, I figured out that Tony was a bigger thief then I had ever imagined. For every book I had, he had three more.

Tony was skimming so much off the top, it's no wonder he was running out of places to store his cash. Except, it wasn't his cash. Someone somewhere must have worked it out.

Tony was a thief, but not a clever one. The amounts he stole were too big. I think he was trying to hide it all, make it all disappear before people came to claim what was theirs.

For a split second, I regretted not taking that piece of ham from his throat; I would have loved nothing more than to see his body stretched naked across his table and whipped.

A bark from outside snapped me out of my trance. I grabbed the books and papers from his desk a nd stuffed them under my arms. Someone had to know what was going on, and I was going to make sure that 'someone' was me. This was my insurance policy.

A second bark.

I ran down the stairs and swung the iron door open scanning the street. No cars.

I sprinted not looking behind me. Spots appeared by my side; he ran, his tongue flapping in the night air.

He disappeared not far from the car wash. I guess he had crawled into his burrow. I kept looking behind me—waiting scanning. I unlocked the door to the car wash with unsteady hands and rushed to my room.

My heart drumming an unsteady beat, I tucked the books in the cavity I had made myself a year ago. I grabbed my bat and fell on my bed, wiping sweat from my brow.

If you want, you can label me a monster. Maybe I am. I didn't feel a fucking thing watching that fat fucker die. Well, that's not true. I felt happiness; a warm trickle of joy spread through me as his body wobbled and shook.

Two days before my twentieth birthday, Tony had given me the second-best gift of my life.

Freedom.

The news spread like a rash. They said Tony was found that morning, stiff and blue and bulging. But I knew it was much earlier than that.

Someone banged on my door.

It was early, too early. I rubbed sleep from my eyes and opened the door to find a tired looking Salvatore on the other side.

"What?" I snapped at him. But I knew what, and I suspected he knew, too.

"The boss is dead." Salvatore showed as much emotion as a rock.

"What?"

"Tony. They found him dead in his office this morning."

"What? How?" I gave an Oscar-worthy performance.

"He choked to death—on a fucking sandwich." Salvatore's upper lip twitched.

I tried. I really did. But the smirk that crossed my face was totally out of my control. It stretched and stretched like it had a will all of its own, and I coughed hiding the laughter that rose in my throat. I wasn't giving any condolences. I had none.

"So, what now?"

"Now? It's business as usual. The funeral will be tomorrow. Joe Romano is coming."

"Lupe?"

"Yeah, he's probably going to hang around after."

It was a warning. He didn't have to tell me.

I nodded. My heart pounded in my chest. If I had to go up against anyone, I hated for it to be against Joe 'The Builder' Romano. But, if that's what it took to wash my hands clean and walk away, I would tear him down and walk right through him and every other fucker they sent.

"Get dressed, boss. We have work to do." I hated when he did that—call me boss then tell me what to do like I was a child.

When you're young, you don't really admit to yourself that you're a kid. You feel like a man because you think you know what a man is made of. You think you know what it takes, the sacrifices, the cost. Someone had to mature, make tough decisions, be the adult. So, I thought I was a man because I stepped up when I was a kid; because, I watched a man die; because, I've been with women; because, I ate shit for years and just digested it.

What I realised, was all that shit gave me tools; tools I needed to sharpen; tools I needed to understand how to use; tools that would burn me or save me. When it came to playing with the big boys, I wasn't all that I thought I was.

Until, eventually, I was.

———

The funeral home was packed—judges, cops, lawyers, doctors. The elite. I'm pretty sure most of them came just to make sure he was dead. You could hear the collective sigh of relief as they lowered his coffin into the ground and the first grains of earth landed on the wood.

The mild afternoon had little warmth, even as the sun began its decent and filtered through the trees. There were a few audible sniffles, I think they were mostly from his daughters and his mistress. They would all miss his money more than they would ever miss him.

His wife hired a venue for the wake. She didn't want anyone staining her beautiful furniture and handpicked home décor. She played the mourning wife pretty well, but anyone with eyes could see the looks she was exchanging with another man across the room. He would have been no more than five years my senior, and he gave her the kind of look a hungry dog gives his food bowl; he knows where to get it from he just needs it filled up. Seems like Tony and his wife liked them young. The thought made the bile rise to my throat. I wished I could dig him out just so I could kick his fucking face in.

I stayed long enough for everyone to see my face and to give my condolences to Tony's wife. I spotted Rita. A flurry of butterflies took flight in my belly. She looked fresh and happy, and I felt almost relieved. Her new boyfriend hung on her like a coat. He was tall and broad, and his arms looked like they might tear from his suit. When she saw me, she pushed away from him and came over throwing her arms around me.

"You've filled out." She winked at me.

"And you seem unavailable."

"I might make an exception for you." She bit her lower lip and sucked it in, an edge of a smile tugging at her lips.

I could feel my cock twitch, my mind reeling to that night in the car four years back. Of course, I've been with others since Rita but none have left such a scorching mark on me as she did.

Before I could answer, her boyfriend walked over. His

eyes assessed me top to bottom, and I could see his shoulders bunch up and his jaw flex.

"I have to go. Nice seeing you, Rita."

When I turned around and left, I heard him ask her who the loser was. I rolled my eyes and stepped outside. I looked for Salvatore, hoping for a lift, but he was too busy with his arms around two different women.

I spotted Alice; of course, she was there. Like a scavenger feeding on the corpse, she had her arm hooked around a man in a fitted suit. His face was familiar; he was probably on Tony's pay list. She would make enough today to see her through next week. I felt dirty again.

I started walking aimlessly. I wasn't afraid of the future, not that I ever really was. The future was always written out for me, but now I had a chance to change all that. I just had to get home and look at those books. Really look at them, study them and read between the lines to find out what Tony was really doing. Then, I would change everything.

When I got home, it was dark. I grabbed Spots' food bowl and went to sit my vigil. I didn't have to wait long. Spots showed up and walked right up to me. He ate his food, wagging his tail and, when he was done, he sat right by me allowing me to scratch his head and pat him. His mouth reeked as he panted with joy, and his matted fur stuck between my fingers. But fuck it if he didn't make me smile. When I stood up, he didn't run off.

"Hey buddy, do you want to sleep inside tonight?" I held the door open and waited. I could see his little brain tick over. I walked into the door and held it open. "Well?"

He looked down the street and then back into the lit-up room. With a galloping dart, he came inside.

At last.

Happy birthday to me.

PART V

Ten Years Later

I'm going to have to jump ahead for a while. Not because what happened isn't important; It is. There is so much to tell. But we can get back to all that later, because I think I've given you enough of my pain. I need to breathe a little. Maybe you do, too.

So, I'll give you the nutshell and promise to fill you in on the details later on.

All you need to know for now is, during that time, I did all that needed to be done. There was so much dust stirred up from Tony's shit storm, it took a long time for it all to settle and get cleaned up. I did what had to be done. I paid the price. I became a man.

I changed sheets. I went to work. I cried, curled up like a baby, weak and agonised, starving for something. Anything.

I drank into empty nights and lost myself in chrome and tools and slick black oil. I went home. I bought the shop, made it mine. My own. I didn't owe a thing to anyone. Although, a few still thought differently. It scared me. That fear plagued me. Still does, even now.

Alice got clean. We started meeting for coffee once a month. That you already know…

———

It already felt like a long day. Any day I saw Alice automatically turned long and agonising. I bought her coffee. After three years of being clean, she finally allowed herself a cup. No sugar though.

I half listened as she prattled on about her new job. She was a cleaner for some hotel, changed the sheets and brushed the toilets. She put on a bit of weight, and her hair wasn't so stringy any more. Her skin looked better too. But, if I was to be honest, I haven't seen her happy in years.

Not really.

We talked about crap, skirting over all the real issues. I just kept waiting for the other shoe to drop, for her to let go of everything and fall back into old habits, to go sit on that bench with some fucker's hand up her pussy, score her ten dollars, and let her dealer pimp her out so she can get her hit.

I tried not to think about it as she told me about the rancid rooms she cleaned, or how lovely the weather was. She asked about Spots, and her skew grin was almost sad. Her stained teeth were crooked and unstable. She lost another one. She looks way too fucking old for her age. In fact, I'm surprised she's made it to the ripe ol' age of forty-nine.

"You did good, kiddo." She kissed me on the cheek with chapped lips. I cringed at her touch.

"Yeah. See you, Alice."

I gave her some cash and left. I used to give her food, but

she never ate it. She gave it to her friends, the hungry ones. So, I started giving her cash. I knew she would hold onto that —maybe even pay rent. Alice was on her own. She was a grown ass woman and could do what she wanted.

I left her on the bench and walked over to the shop. The spring sun was warm, there was colour everywhere, new blooms and new life. My mind drifted to the work that had to be done.

We had two BMWs, a Lexus, and a Maserati that were due out that evening. The few others on the floor could be worked on later that week.

I had rebuilt the shop to be an exclusive luxury car repair garage. I made a name for myself; one that I built from the ashes of Tony's memory.

The boys were already hands deep inside the cars when I arrived. They mumbled a hello, and I went to my room for a quick change. I took my old childhood room back, made it bigger and a bit more comfortable. I knocked all the walls down and rebuilt. Those old walls had too many memories, too many haunted eyes and silent cries. I didn't want to be surrounded by them.

Work helped. My mind was clearer when all I had to think about were screws and engines, clutches and pipes. In truth, I wanted the day to be over. I longed to get back to my bike. She was so near completion that I could cry.

The boys left at closing time, and I did a quick end of day calculation. I knew I had some orders to fulfil, but they could wait till morning.

My fingers itched to work on my Harley. When I first laid my eyes on that broken husk ten years earlier, I never antici- pated it would take so long to bring her to life. But war has casualties and she was mine; stashed away in the darkness for years until I could find her again, repossess her. All I wanted was to get that engine roaring, tear down the road, feel those vibrations between my legs, shooting up my body —becoming one with the machine. Just thinking about it gave me a hard on.

The new exhaust pipe arrived that morning. Once I install it, she would be just about done. The ripple effect on the pipe were like waves beneath my fingers as I stripped away the plastic packaging. Spots paced around the empty box, sniffing the contents, his tongue hanging out, his tail wagging like a windscreen wiper during a storm.

"Yeah, buddy. I'm excited too."

I sat on the concrete floor, my ass getting used to the cold hardness, when I heard the door open and slam shut. It was followed by the sucking of air. I smirked. They always react that way when that door slams.

"We're closed. Come back tomorrow." I didn't bother looking up. I was just where I wanted to be.

"I was told you may have a job for me?" Her voice rang, soft and sweet, against the harsh cold walls. I turned to look at the intruder.

She wore knee-high, black, leather boots that showed off just enough leg before her black skirt covered the rest. My eyes travelled the length of her slim torso, which was wrapped up in a leather jacket. Her brown hair cascaded in waves across her shoulders. Her lips shone in a deep red hue. Her hazel eyes rested on Spots, who was wagging his tail.

"Hey boy." She smiled at him. I stood up wiping my hands on my jeans.

"Leave her alone. Go to your room." Spots ignored me and bounded against her leg.

"Don't worry about him. He's gorgeous." She squatted and patted his head, letting him lick her palms.

"Spots! Go, now." He froze for a second then scooted out of the room. I shouldn't have yelled at him, but I would apologise later.

"You didn't have to, I really didn't mi—"

"Who are you and what do you want?" I was harsh and curt.

"Oh, my name is Mia." She offered me a shaky smile; I had clearly knocked the wind out of her sail. "I was told you might have work for me?"

"And, who told you that?"

"Stephano."

I grimaced at the mention of his name. "How do you know him?" I raised an eyebrow; she didn't look like the kind of girl to hang around the likes of him. Then again, what the fuck do I know? I've known her all of three seconds, and I was about to un-know her.

"We're related."

"Poor you."

"It's a distant relationship."

"Doesn't make it any better."

"No, guess not." She cocked her head and the gesture made me smile. Or maybe it was the way she swung her hip and crossed her arms. I was suddenly noticing too many things about this woman.

"Look, I'm not sure what that piece of shit told you, but I'm not hiring."

"But, I need a job."

"So, go find one elsewhere. I'm sure you can wait tables or answer phones somewhere."

"I've tried."

"Try some more. I have nothing for you." She was persistent, but I was all out of charity.

"Please, just give me a shot."

"I just told you; I'm not hiring."

"Please," her eyes welled with tears, "I'm desperate."

"Not my problem." I wanted to turn my back on her, but my legs wouldn't spin and my body wouldn't co-operate. Then my mouth and brain stopped communicating and words came flowing out. "Unless you can work on transmissions, I can't really help you."

She blinked away the unshed tears, and her lips twitched with a hint of a smile. "Well, I guess that depends, is there a delayed vehicle response when you shift from park to reverse? Or is the transmission slipping when the car is shifting gears? Or is it the shakes? Or is it leaking? Or—"

"Okay, okay. So, you know a bit about transmissions."

"I know everything there is to know."

"Is that right?" My heart was suddenly pounding, and I brushed the hair out of my face.

"Why don't you test me out? I'll come tomorrow. Give me any car, and I'll show you what I can do." Suddenly I had some very unholy thoughts as to what this woman could do, and not just to cars.

"Like I said, I'm not hiring." This needed to be shut down now.

"Please." She took a step forward, and her perfume wafted towards me. She peeled off her jacket to reveal a singlet below. It showed off a delicate black outline of a rose tattoo.

My stomach coiled and I had to fight a sudden urge to strip the rest of her clothes off and see what else her skin hid. Her jacket landed on the floor with a muted thud, and she grabbed the wrench I had discarded when she walked in. I didn't know what her intentions were. Did she think she would convince me by tightening some screws? Either way, she wasn't going to work for me.

I grabbed her wrist and stopped her advance, wanting to keep her away from the bike. "Stop."

I released her and held out my hand. She held my gaze for a full second, the flecks in her eyes burning. She placed the wrench in my palm, her fingers trailing along my skin, leaving hot tingles in their wake. She lingered there for just a second as her big eyes searched mine. I turned away and sucked in a deep breath.

"Look, um—what did you say your name was again?"

"Mia. Mia Rizzi."

"Mia, right. Look—"

"Please." She cut me off and the fear in her voice tore me up inside. I have known desperation and, although I didn't know her story, I knew what fear tasted like.

I stepped back, the sweetness of her perfume overpowering, making me dizzy. I rubbed my temples and sighed.

"Can you manage accounts, do inventory...that sort of thing?"

"Well yeah, I can, but I was hoping you'd let me work on the floor."

"It's the office or nothing."

"Is it because I'm a girl?" Her eyebrows knitted together and she pouted. I wanted to suck that pout right off her face.

I cleared my throat, "Yes."

"That's sexist."

"It's to do with workplace efficiency."

"I don't understand."

I sighed. "You're going to be too much of a distraction." There, I said it. And I didn't get the reaction I thought I was going to get. I'm really not sure why I thought she'd be flattered. Was I even giving her a compliment?

Shit, I needed help talking to women. But right then, I had another problem—the tiny, little dynamite stick that was walking towards me.

Her hips swung just a little as she closed the distance between us, her skirt hiking an inch up her creamy, smooth thigh. Suddenly, my mouth was too dry and swallowing became too hard.

"That's sexist. It's not my problem men can't keep their dicks in their pants."

"But it's going to become my problem! I need them to work, not stare at you—" I gestured like an idiot at her body, "your body." I felt sweat on my forehead. I felt sixteen again, uncertain and clumsy. Who was this woman?

"I bet if you were working in an all women's factory, you'd hate to be put in the office." Did she just give me a compliment or call me a girl?

"The job opening is for an office job only. Take it or leave it."

"Fine!" She scowled, crossing her arms again.

"Fine!" I gritted my teeth, as she flicked locks of hair over her shoulder, exposing her long neck and the swell of her breasts.

"When can I start?" Her eyes hovered on mine.

"Come tomorrow morning and I'll show you around."

Her scowl dissolved into a relieved smile that lit up her face, "Thank you." Mia whirled around and bent over to pick up her discarded jacket.

Her skirt hitched up as she bent down.

Now I tried, maybe not as hard as I should have, but fuck it; I couldn't keep my eyes off those legs of hers. The skirt hitched up a few more notches, and beneath I could see the traces of black panties.

My cock fought against my jeans, which all of a sudden felt too tight. She turned back to me and gave me a final thanks before the door slammed shut behind her.

As soon as that door closed, it felt as if all the air was sucked out of the room with her. Like a tornado had just raged inside, I felt wrecked. My heart thumped and I adjusted my pants, my cock seeking what was no longer there. Except for her smell, she left that shit everywhere.

My mind felt cloudy and turbulent. What did I just do? This desire that Mia had stirred up in me felt dangerous and raw. I needed to clear my head; I needed the world to make sense; I needed to fuck the desire for Mia right out of my system, and then I needed to fire her.

I pulled out my phone and called Valentina. She was always good for a quick release. She would let me violate her in the most indecent of ways. I could leave her, wasted, unapologetic, and clearheaded.

She answered the phone after the first ring. Her needy voice grated against my nerves. I knew she wanted me. I knew she wanted so much more of me—all of me. But I didn't feel the same. I didn't feel anything at all. She was just a warm body, nothing more. A rag doll that let me take out all of my anger and frustrations, a desperate thing that allowed me to do the worst to it and beg me for more. I didn't feel bad for her.

When we first met, I told her there weren't going to be feelings involved. It was just a physical need being fulfilled. I needed her to be my release valve whenever I was angry or lonely or lost. The deeper I sank, the rougher I became and the more she allowed me. It was cruel. But all I had to give, was only what I could take from her.

I parked outside her house, and I could see the lights from underneath her dark curtains. I could envision her half naked and ready, begging for me, willing me to do what I wanted, taking it, and allowing it. It was pitiful.

My mind filled with thoughts of Mia. Her smart mouth, pale skin, and that delicate rose tattoo. I wanted to colour that rose with her blood as I bit into her. My cock twitched at the thought. I hit the steering wheel with both hands and screeched away.

When Valentina called me an hour later, I let the phone ring. After the eighth try, she gave up. I sucked down the last of my beer and left it on the counter. I peeled off my shirt. My body ached with the day's weight. My hands burned with small scratches, and my nails were black with oil. I wanted to wash the day from my body; I wanted to wash away the thoughts of Alice and Valentina—they both stained my soul like grease.

I stood under the hot deluge and pumped some body wash into my hands. I worked the liquid into a lather and washed myself, trying to cleanse my thoughts. Till they landed on Mia and the way her skirt travelled up her thigh.

My cocked twitched again and this time it asked for attention. I lathered more soap onto my hand and began to stroke my hardening shaft while seeing Mia's hot-red lips, imagining them around my cock.

Her long slim legs wrapped around me.

My head buried in her neck, her perfume enveloping me as I had her.

Fucked her.

Took her.

Claimed her.

My stomach coiled as pleasure built in my core, my cock harder, swelling in my hand. With a final pump I jerked, releasing myself over the shower tiles. I groaned at the release, holding onto the wall, catching my breath.

I rinsed myself and towelled off, feeling an anti-climax. Orgasming in my hand with little foreplay felt satisfying, but not particularly pleasurable. Just empty.

That night I was plagued by dreams of black lips and red roses.

I was only halfway through my coffee when the door slammed shut.

I heard a faint 'shit' as it echoed through the shop. My lips twitched at the sound and, despite my protests, my heart fluttered in my chest.

Her heels clanged against the concrete floor, and I stepped out of the kitchen to greet her. I gritted my teeth as I took her in.

Her face stretched in a grin when she saw me crossing the workshop towards her. "You're early." I admonished her.

The smile faltered a little. "Isn't it better than being late?"

I didn't have time to argue or explain. "Come this way." I turned my back to her and walked towards the staircase.

I led her into the office. Since taking the business over, I made some changes, destroyed memories, and created a clean slate.

Whereas Tony used to hide behind small windows and closed curtains, I made sure everyone knew I was watching. I tore down the walls, shattered his tiny glass panes, and replaced his secrets with wall to ceiling windows.

The office was sparsely furnished with a large handmade mahogany desk. All the paperwork was stored in a cabinet shelf against one wall, a water cooler and drink station rested against the other.

"You can work here today."

"And where will you work?"

"I'll be downstairs." My jaw clenched, thinking I saw disappointment flash in her eyes.

I logged on to the computer and gestured for her to sit. She slung her handbag over the chair and removed her leather jacket, hanging it over the back of the chair. My breath stalled as she shimmied into the chair, her mini skirt catching against the leather, riding up her legs.

I tore my eyes from her legs and returned my attention to the screen. "Are you familiar with Quick Accounts Solutions?"

"Yeah, we used to use it on the farm." I frowned and waited, but she didn't give me anymore.

I leaned over the chair, clicking the mouse.

"Ok, here it is." I was leaning so low my head was right beside hers. I could feel the heat radiating from her cheeks. I caught a whiff of her sweet perfume. It wasn't nauseatingly sweet, but more like pine and freshly cut grass. She was a rose and I was suddenly attracted to her with the kind of reckless trance that brings a butterfly to nectar.

I rubbed the back of my neck and tried to concentrate on

the screen, but my eyes kept flicking to her unbuttoned blouse, the show of skin above her knees, the wave of her hair.

"Do you understand?" I heard myself talking.

"Yes." Mia reached for the mouse. Her hand snaking along mine, skin against skin, heat sliding up my arm. Her fingers fluttered over the plastic buttons as my own lingered. She turned to face me, and our eyes locked. I could feel her hot breath on my face, her lips glossy and red. I pulled my hand away from the mouse, and my fingers found their way to her gentle face. I swiped a strand of her hair, tucking it behind her ear—seemingly innocent. I ignored my chugging heart. I ignored every screaming thought and burning desire. Until I was too weak; until I was but a hairsbreadth away from stealing a kiss, from firing Mia, from losing my mind.

The sound of the roller door rattled through the workshop, slicing the tension. I yanked my hand away and sprung up like a spring that'd been wound too tight. Mia turned back to the screen, her cheeks flushed. I needed air. I needed to get away from the slew of thoughts in my head.

The guys walked into the workshop and glanced up at the office. They froze mid-step as they noticed Mia in my office. They grinned, then walked in as one.

"I'll introduce you to the guys and show you the storeroom. You'll have to print out the inventory lists and make sure you fulfil them."

"Okay." She sounded breathy.

I walked out of the office, assuming she was behind me. I had to get away from her.

I took the stairs two at a time. I needed more distance, quicker. I needed her to catch up, to be nearer. When I stepped onto the floor, three sets of eyes peered at me. Their cocked heads and smirks all disappeared as soon as Mia appeared beside me.

"This is Mia, Stephano's... cousin." It didn't have to be

true. No one would touch anything that was related to that mad man. Any trace of interest or jeering fell from their faces, and their eyes were suddenly fixed on anything but her. "She will do some office work around here while we catch up on the backlog." There was a general murmur of agreement.

I turned to Mia and she didn't look bothered by their looks, all straight backed and casual like she owned the fucking place. It was hot as hell. Maybe that's why it bothered me so much.

"Meet Romeo, Leo and Joey." She extended her hand and, like servants before their queen, they each stepped forward and shook her hand, almost bowing.

I have to admit, I was almost relieved to see them react to her that way. Maybe she wasn't that special after all, just another body with round parts. I ground my teeth at the thought, knowing I was lying to myself.

"Get to work. That Hyundai needs to be done today. I'll finish showing Mia around, and I'll be down soon."

"Yes boss." They chimed and dispersed.

"This way." I marched off to the back room and yanked the door open. My hand searched the wall, and the lights exploded to life in a blinding flash. The storeroom seemed endless; shelves upon shelves heaped with parts, bolts, oils and tyres.

I spent the better part of an hour showing her that storeroom, knowing I was wasting time. With a routine inventory due in three days, there would be plenty of time for a detailed tour and explanations. But I wanted to be near her, appreciate how her delicate features fit in with all this hard coldness.

When I couldn't waste any more time, I sent her upstairs and went to work with the boys. I needed my hands inside a metal body. Lifting, tuning, and fixing, keeping my mind firmly on the job and away from her.

For the first time since I took the place over, I stayed out of my office the entire day; I even ate lunch with the boys. I noticed how much more we completed. There were no interruptions, not one—not a single phone call, not a single delivery. I dived into the machine and there I remained. Now that I had resurfaced, a shiver ran down my spine. What the hell has she been doing with all my customers? I clenched my fists and stormed up the stairs. Why the hell did I relinquish so much control to a complete stranger? I was a fool.

I barged into my office, her eyes shot to me, and she flashed me her teeth. I was about to start shouting, swearing, and asking questions when she held up her hand and pointed at the phone.

"Sure thing, Mrs. Rogers. The car will be ready by Tuesday." She nodded, "Yes well, unfortunately, when they removed the carburettor and opened the bowl, they found that it was completely corroded." She looked at me and nodded into the phone, "Yes, it's a standard rebuild and assembly and, as I've just said, it will be ready by Tuesday."

My face went slack staring at her, listening to her. Mia knew what she was talking about, and I bet she knew almost as much about cars and engines as I did. I would have to find out where she learned everything. And if I could get her to cover up that sweet, sweet little body of hers, I might even let her to come down to the workshop. I sat on the edge of the table and admired her, her confidence, her spark.

She was very bad news.

"Okay, thank you. See you then." She smiled down at the phone and placed the receiver back. Her attention returned to me and her smile widened.

"Everything okay, boss man?"

"You're fired," I said and stood up, my jaw a fixed line.

"What? Why?"

"Mrs. Rogers's car will not be done by Tuesday; we still have two cars to get done."

Mia pushed off her chair and took three long strides to close the distance between us. "That car will be done by Tuesday, because you'll work on it tomorrow. There's an extra set of hands on the floor, and I've been busy answering phones all day and cleaning up your mess."

"What mess?"

She dismissed my question with a wave of her hand. "You need to be down there, and I need to be up here."

Her face was flushed and her eyes flared. She had this whole damn thing figured out.

"Fine! Keep the job, but you'll need to be here on Saturday for stock take. So, don't make any plans."

"Fine." She stormed back to the chair and grabbed her jacket and shoulder bag. "I'm done for today." Mia marched to the door, anger vibrating from her body. "You're welcome!"

I was furious and totally turned on. This woman was going to be my end, I felt it in my bones.

I was fucked.

———

When I fell out of bed on Saturday morning, I was somewhere between elated and nervous. My entire body felt as if it was vibrating, standing on a precipice, looking down over the abyss. I didn't want to step backwards, and I didn't want to fall over. I needed to find a safe way across.

I did all the morning things a person does and headed up to my office. I had been avoiding it throughout the week. I tried to maintain my balance as I walked in. Even though Mia left almost eighteen hours ago, traces of her smell hung in the air. She left behind a hundred little reminders that she had spent the week at work; meaningless doodles on the edges of papers, an empty coffee cup with an imprint of her lips, some kind of plant that she brought in with her to 'liven the place up.'

I plummeted into my chair, scanning the room. My eyes landed on green leaves; the thing leered at me, taunted me. It got to spend the entire day looking at her, listening to her voice, and watching her while I was hauling engines and tightening bolts. I didn't mind the work. It meant my mind was focused on one thing only, and I kept telling myself that it wasn't Mia.

Her work was meticulous. All the numbers added up. Her booking system surpassed mine, and she had somehow made the place look brighter. But, I already knew all that. I snapped the coffee cup off the table as I headed out of the office. I left the office door open hoping her scent would disappear, and wishing I could drown in it at the same time.

By the time I was back downstairs, my coffee was barely lukewarm. I choked on the murky liquid and spat it into the sink. I emptied the rest of my cup, rinsed it out and grabbed Mia's. The lipstick stain disappeared beneath the hot water and soap. I tried to erase traces of her in slow circular motions. The cup dripped next to mine on the drying tray, droplets falling and collecting then linking to one another, creating a little pool of water in the silver basin.

Spots perked up. With pricked ears, his head shot up and he sniffed the air. A second later the heavy door slammed shut. Spots bolted from his bed and ran over towards the noise.

Mia appeared in the kitchen a moment later, Spots bounding and leaping around her.

"Hi buddy. Yeah, it's nice to see you too." She patted him on the head and rubbed his neck.

"Spots, go away." He gave me a sulky look and skulked back to his bed.

"Why are you so mean to him?"

"Why don't you mind your own fucking business?" She

flinched. I probably shouldn't have been so harsh to her but, truth be told, she knew nothing about Spots and me. And, as much as I needed and loved that fucking mutt, I just wanted her undivided attention.

"Let's go, we have a lot of work to do." She dropped her bag on the plastic kitchen table and walked by me towards the storeroom.

She stood in the door frame, her hands on her hips, her eyes sweeping the shelves, the gravity of our task settling on her shoulders. She wore tight jeans and a light blue singlet, the strap of her black bra jutting out slightly beneath the cotton fabric.

"What are you staring at?" She caught me looking.

"Do you have any spare clothes?"

"No, why?"

"Cause you're going to ruin those." I shrugged, playing the nice guy.

"How? I thought we were counting parts."

"We are. But they're dirty, and oily, and sharp. We have some spare overalls."

"Sure, I'd appreciate it." She gave me a little smile.

I found the smallest pair, knowing they would still be way too big and handed them over. "You can change in my room. That's the door over in the corner," Her eyes followed my pointed finger, "The one that says 'no entry.'"

"You live here?"

"Yes." I could see on her face that she had more questions, but I shut her down. "Don't touch anything." I slipped off the silver chain that hung around my neck and handed it over to her. The key dangling from the end.

I watched as she took tentative steps towards the door, looking over her shoulder, uncertainty written all over her features. I nodded. I don't know why, maybe I thought she was still asking for permission.

I knew what she would find in there; an empty space

where Spots' bed usually lay, my desk littered with piles of unfinished paperwork, my bed made up and neat, and maybe a few clothes lying around. I cringed at the thought of her seeing it. Not because it was dirty or unkempt but because it was so meagre, so little. I mean, it's always been good enough for me. I needed nothing more, but what would Mia think?

The door closed behind her. My stomach turned and my heart thudded like a drum in my chest. I imagined her stripping her clothes away, her half-naked body sitting on the edge of my bed, her scent mingling with mine. I brushed my hands over my face in an attempt to quench my desires.

When she came out, her hair was in a messy bun and she was swimming in the oversized coverall. "Smells much better in there than it does out here."

I swallowed her words and sighed; this wasn't going to work.

"Just...stand there." I looked around until I found a length of rope. "Stand still."

"What are you doing?" She eyed the length of rope in my hand.

"It's too loose. You'll get caught on something and possibly get hurt, I just don't have time to play doctor today."

"I bet you'd make a great doctor; in fact, I think most of your patients would be happy to get hurt just to have your hands on them."

I froze for a second at her remark. A smirk spread on her lips.

I stalked around her and fisted the loose fabric in my hand, gathering as much of it as I could, bunching it in my hand. I pulled tightly until most of the fabric around her body didn't hang too loosely. I tied the excess in a tight ball. "How does that feel?"

"Fine."

"Roll up your sleeves. They're too long."

"Can you help me? Whenever I do it, they keep unrolling."

"Sure."

She extended her hands and I grabbed the sleeve. I rolled it, one neat fold after another, exposing her delicate arms. My fingers brushed her skin, and the familiar tingle of touching her sent my body reeling. I ground my teeth as I rolled the second sleeve, perhaps a little less meticulously. As I rolled it for the last time, my finger brushed her arm and our eyes met. Her gaze pinned me and, for what felt like a full moment, we stood frozen.

Staring.

Longing.

I broke away, and a pang shot to my heart as I saw her face twist. I shook off the feeling and walked towards the storage room. "Let's go. We have a very long day ahead."

I could see her eyes trying to roll to the back of her head as I went on and on about how we slotted inventory; how we assigned parts to a location based on the part's movement and physical characteristics, such as size and weight. Her eyes never left my face as I explained counting and entering and mismatch possibilities. Something was holding her attention and it wasn't the conversation. My heart wanted to beat faster, to get excited. Emotional, attached maybe, but I shut it down. There was no room in there for anyone else.

"Do you understand?"

"What?"

Had she listened to a single word I said? "Just follow my lead."

"Yes, boss."

"Don't call me that." I shot her a scathing look, and she recoiled. I almost wanted to apologise. Almost.

"What would you like me to call you?"

"Gabriel."

"Ok, Gabriel." My name sounded so sweet on her lips, I wanted to suck that honey nectar right from them.

Instead I pulled out the first box of 32mm nuts, brought

up the product ID number on the iPad and started counting, nodding to the 40mm nuts right next to them. Without missing a beat, she grabbed the box and started counting.

It was quiet work, which is why I usually loved doing it. The silence filled up the emptiness inside me. And yet, today everything felt too loud, too full.

I was totally aware of her—all of her. Her shallow breathing, the rise and fall of her chest. The way her fingers moved through cold, hard parts as they clinked around in the boxes, tinkering and rolling. How her lips moved as she counted; glossy, full lips that she would lick or bite every time she'd lose count or remember something. How meticulously she worked and how hard, her forehead gleaming with a sheen of sweat.

Every now and then she'd catch me looking, her eyes widened and she turned her head away as if she was the one that was caught. My lips twitched with the thought.

My arms ached and my back strained as I reached for more parts—box after box—meandering through the shelves. The deeper we ventured into the storeroom, the narrower the space became, the more cramped, the thicker the air, the darker the room.

The last aisle was crammed with heavy, underutilised parts that were covered in dust. I knew exactly how many of each item was there. I could see by the layered dust that nothing had been touched since the last time I was here.

It was so tight and narrow, and Mia stood so close, too close. The smell of her shampoo covered every inch of the space. Like the dust, it settled onto everything, infecting every part of the storeroom. Of me. I was like a hound with a scent, and all I wanted to do was chase that fucking rabbit.

I reached for the collection of safety bars. The weight dipped the top shelf and, in truth, I should have left it, called it a day and filled out the rest of the paperwork. Alone. I should have sent her home. I should have tightened the leash around my own neck. Mia was a distraction; a terrible, wonderful distraction.

Like in a slow-motion movie, the bars rolled out of their box. With only split seconds to react, I pushed Mia out of the way. I could hear my elbows connect with her ribs, and the air gushing out of her lungs as she fell away. The heavy metal rods fell down like metallic rain, and two collided with my face with solid thuds. The pain was searing and instantaneous. I could feel the hot flow of blood from my wounds as my legs collapsed beneath me, and I smashed into the shelves with force. The rods fell to the ground, ringing and clinking as they hit the concrete.

I sucked in a deep breath, trying to refill my lungs with air. My head throbbed and I could feel the rush of blood as it made its way down my cheek. I swiped it away just to feel the next rivulet follow.

I groaned as I turned my head looking for Mia. She was pinned to the opposite side of the narrow aisle, her hands above her head trying to make herself disappear into the wall.

"Are you okay?" My words stumbled from my mouth as I tried to catch my breath.

She let her hands drop from her face and scanned herself, patting her body down. "Yes, I'm fi…" her eyes fell on my face. "Shit, you're bleeding."

"I'm fine." I kept wiping at my face, my hand stained red.

"You need to have that looked at." She walked over to me and extended her hand.

"It's fine." I growled at her.

"Come on." She didn't move. I stuffed my hand into her outstretched palm and a shiver went through me. I pulled myself up and Mia led us out of the storeroom. The room was striped with long shadows as the sun made its way beneath the horizon.

Mia took long, purposeful strides toward the kitchenette.

Concern marred her beautiful features and, despite the blood coursing down my face, I couldn't take my eyes off her hips as they swayed with purpose.

"Sit!" She pushed me into a chair and turned on the light, the flash searing my eyes. "Let me have a look at you." She hovered above me, her lower lip tipped with worry.

"I'm fine." I tried for the third time.

"You're not! Where's the first aid kit?"

I pointed to the cupboard. Mia rummaged around and rose again with the red first aid box.

She opened the box and dug inside sighing. She took out a bottle and some gauze. Always meticulous. I watched as she placed everything in a neat line, preparing herself. She unbuttoned the coveralls and slipped her arms from the long sleeves.

"I prefer taking a girl out to dinner before I get her to take her clothes off."

"Somehow, I find that hard to believe." She scoffed, turned to the sink and washed her hands.

"That hurts."

"More than that cut on your head?"

"Much more." Despite the sarcasm, my heart still swelled at her concern.

Mia came over and stood over me. "This is going to sting a little."

Ever so gently, she put the alcohol-soaked gauze to my forehead. I hissed and grabbed her wrist pulling her away.

"Shit."

"Stop being such a baby." She yanked her hand, pulling it free and dabbed at my wound. "How's that?" Her touch had softened, her eyes lingered on mine, then flicked back to her work.

"It's fine," I swallowed hard. "Thank you." My heart thumped like a crazed lunatic's fist against an asylum window.

"That's a deep cut. You're going to need stitches."

"Don't worry about it."

"I'm not done with you! Do you have a needle and thread somewhere?"

I sucked in a deep breath; she wasn't going to let this go.

"I have one in my room. Let me go and get it." I made to stand up, but her hand landed on my chest and pushed me down.

"Sit down!" Her eyes blazed and her nostrils flared, she wasn't taking any shit. "Where is it?"

"I don't want you rummaging around in my things."

"What can you possibly be hiding?"

I wish she hadn't asked that. "Top drawer of my chest of drawers," I grumbled.

She held out her hand for the key. "It's unlocked."

"Hold that in place till I get back." She placed my hand over the gauze and retreated out of the room at a sprinter's pace.

As soon as she stepped out of the kitchenette I hissed in pain. That rod hit me harder than I was ready to admit. I guess a couple of stitches were better than a cracked skull. I leaned back against the wall shutting my eyes.

"I found all your skeletons." My mouth twitched.

"You wouldn't be back if you had." My eyes opened into slits.

The touch of her hand on mine was delicate and unexpected. She peeled my hand back from my wound, and I let it drop by my side. "You don't happen to have any aesthetic lying around do you?"

"It's not that kind of establishment?"

"The kind that puts people to sleep?"

I guffawed at her crack. "The kind that holds unnecessary drugs."

"Well, are you going to be a brave boy while I stitch you up?"

"There's no way you're coming near me with that needle." I opened one eye and peered at her threading black thread through the eye of the needle.

"Relax, I know what I'm doing."

"How?"

"I used to stitch the animals back at the farm."

"You keep mentioning this farm, tell me about it."

"No."

I bit the inside of my lip. "Your voice will help me keep my mind off the fact that you're about to stab me with that thing." I closed my eyes and waited.

And then my lungs filled with her scent. Not so much the fruity artificial scent, but hers—her musky sweat and woodsy skin, like the sun had crawled beneath it and left its rays behind, as if all the hay and grass in the meadows sat just on the fringes of her skin.

"Don't move, I'd hate to stab you in the eye." The way she said it made me smile. In another life, I might have burst out laughing. What was she doing to me?

My hand clenched at my side and I felt her hips brush against mine as she positioned herself.

"Are you ready?"

"Talk."

She pinched the wound and I hissed as the prick of the needle bit into my skin. The sting lasted seconds, followed by the strange sensation of a foreign object moving under my skin.

"I had two horses, Jigsaw and Cookie."

"Should I guess which one you named?" I smirked, pretending I didn't feel the tug of the thread as it pulled through my skin. I winced while she ignored my remark.

"It wasn't a ranch, if that's what you're about to ask next, the horses came later. We were dairy farmers first." She pushed the needle through a second time. My hand found her hip, like a crutch. I grabbed on to it and dug into her skin as she tugged on the thread. I heard her soft gasp as my fingers found her flesh just beyond her shirt. Completely unintentional, totally gratifying. Her skin was just as soft as I had imagined, flawless. I shouldn't have lingered, I shouldn't have enjoyed my fingers there or the feel of her, but I couldn't help myself. My cock responded, bulging and swelling, wanting.

"Talk." I needed the distraction, even as her needle poked me for the third time, even as my fingers brushed her skin ever so gently, even as my heart slammed in my chest.

"My dad owned the farm. We had about 120 head of cattle at any given time. Milking cows and shovelling shit isn't the most glorious job, but looking after those animals with their big brown eyes and wet noses, it was beautiful."

I squeezed her again as she tugged at the thread.

"How do you know so much about cars?"

"The tractor broke down a lot, and my dad was a collector. He taught me everything I know."

"Why did you leave?"

"You're all done." Without warning, she stepped out of my grasp and the heat of her body was just a memory etched on the periphery of my being.

"Keep your eyes closed."

They felt so heavy, I don't think I would have been able to open them even if I tried.

I heard the water running and then felt the warmth. The hot, wet towel slid across my face. She was gentle in a way I had never known before, washing traces of blood from my face. It felt almost religious.

"You need to lie down."

"I may have a concussion."

"You need to rest. Can you stand up?"

I opened my eyes reluctantly, the light was too bright. Shit, maybe I did have a concussion.

"Take these." She handed me two white pills and a glass of

water. I swallowed and stood up. She took me by the hand and led me to my room.

"You need to lie down."

My eyelids felt heavy and my body tired. She was right. But I didn't want to lie down. My fingers ached with emptiness. They wanted to keep holding on to her flesh, to explore it and discover it. My entire body ached with need. Mia led me to the bed and pushed me gently, urging me to lie down.

I wanted to argue but my mouth was dry and my head heavy. I sank into the bed, feeling a weight by my side.

"Good boy," Mia's voice rang in my ears. "You look after him."

Spots panted in my ear, his dog's breath washed over me and the world turned black.

When I woke up, someone was there. Spots snored gently by my side; uncertainty clouded my thoughts as my body wound tight around itself. I have felt this way before. Unsure. I didn't like that feeling. It reminded me of the times Alice brought men back with her, and they would sneak around searching for money or drugs. Staying out of the way was a skill. Pretending I was still asleep when Alice was getting fucked or beat or high, now that was an art form.

I mastered the art of faking it.

I kept my breathing even, and with every breath turned my head an inch. When I finally saw what had woke me, it was hard to focus on my breathing. It was hard to keep breathing at all.

Mia stood with her back to the bed, the coveralls on the floor. Her skin looked honeyed in the dim light and her black, lacy underwear was stark against it. The black rose bloomed on her shoulder behind the slip of her singlet. She slipped into her jeans and pulled, the material moulding to the perfect contours of her ass. I would have done almost anything in the world to be that pair of jeans.

I shifted on the bed and feigned awakening. She turned startled.

"Sorry," she whispered. "I didn't mean to wake you."

"You didn't." My voice sounded hoarse and full of sleep. "How long have I been asleep?"

"About two hours."

I frowned. "What have you been doing?" I know exactly how I sounded. Suspicious, angry—like an asshole.

The concern vanished from her face, replaced with an ugly snarl. "I finished the stupid inventory." She shoved the iPad at me. "Here you go, boss! See you on Monday."

She stormed out of the room without looking back.

I watched my door slam, it was echoed by the red door banging behind her. Spots shot from the bed and scratched the door.

I sat up and regretted it instantly. My head throbbed. I looked at the iPad in my hand. A yellow post-it note was stuck on the black screen.

Dear Gabriel,
    I finished the inventory.
    Hope your head feels better.
    Mia XX

Two X's? Was I meant to read anything into that? I felt like an asshole. But I had to be. I couldn't give her any indication of how much I wanted her. She could never think that we could ever be more than what we are—a boss and his employee. It would be fooling both of us.

Spots scratched at the door.

"I'm coming, buddy."

Spots bolted to the door, his tail wagging wildly as I pushed it open for him. He leapt outside and sprinted down the road. Pushing away the old fear. He would be fine.

I stepped outside hoping the cool, fresh air would calm the aching in my head and cleanse the myriad of thoughts running rampant in my mind. If anything, the air did the exact opposite. It made every image clearer, every vision more vivid, more alive.

Mia's long legs and round ass, the delicate, hot feel of her skin beneath my fingers. My pulse hammered as I imagine her bent over my bed with my cock inside her, my hands fisting her hair.

I shoved the thought away violently. But it was too late. My body was already on fire, infected by her. The infection spread rapidly and was completely and utterly devastating. It would unravel and destroy all my barriers. I needed to be better protected. Immunised. I needed to push her away, as far away as she'd go. But that was Monday's problem. Till then, I had a raging need that required attention.

"Fuck."

I called for Spots and apologised for the short walk, promising I would make it up to him. I fell onto my bed feeling fifteen again, with no control of my body and thoughts. She had me completely frazzled. I pulled my pants down. I was already hard and swollen, but all I wanted was to savour the feeling, savour the image of her.

I started stroking my shaft in long, soft strokes, allowing the pleasure to rise, the swelling to grow, the need to become an ache. I could feel my threshold nearing. I pumped faster, imagining her lips, the feel of her skin, the curve of her ass. And then, I let myself fall into the pleasure of it, convulsing in a shuddering release. I lay there for a few minutes recovering, then cleaned myself up. I don't remember the last time I'd felt so good giving myself a hand job. I can only imagine what she might bring out in me.

I tried pushing the thought away again. I allowed myself

to drift into a fitful sleep of arched backs on green fields and lips glossy in the sunshine.

PART VI

We skirted around each other, staying in the periphery. Close enough to feel the pull, but far enough to be able to resist the drag. Anytime I was near enough to smell her scent and feel her eyes on me, I was too close. Too close to the sun, too close to burn with desire. Echoes of her touch stained my skin and crawled beneath it —teasing, demanding, wanting more of her warmth. The walls I built around myself became higher, more fortified, more dangerous.

Most people built prisons to keep people in; I had built mine to keep her out.

It was another busy week but, with Mia in the office, we had been getting through the work quickly. She was efficient and proficient, and she scheduled our work so that we were always busy but never snowed under. Always managing to get cars finished just before their deadlines. She ordered parts even before we knew we needed them. She was amazing. She had also completely taken over my office, which was fine. Being on the floor, surrounded by heavy machinery instead of being bogged down by paperwork, was like having my chains broken.

With only a quick oil change remaining on an Alpha Romeo, I sent the boys home early. They would get on the bottle and some whore, and I wouldn't see them again till Monday. The car could wait. I had the whole weekend to take care of it.

I walked upstairs, and the office door was closed. I knocked while opening it, and frowned at myself. Why was I knocking while walking into my own office? She hadn't rearranged a thing—apart from the green tree that had somehow survived this place. But, it all seemed different. Maybe it was because all of it was somehow touched by her perfection.

She lifted her head when I stepped in, and her face broke into a smile. Damn that smile. It threatened to melt everything inside me.

"How did we do this week?'

"Great." Her smile widened and it seemed like she was about to lurch into a speech about numbers and clients and profits. I didn't need her to tell me. She was a great worker but, like everyone else, I didn't trust her as far as I could throw her.

I spent weekends pouring over her work, reading her delicate, round handwriting and sinking in the scent that had saturated the walls of my office. I knew she wasn't stealing— for now. In truth, sifting through her work was a way for me to be closer to her without having to hear her ringing voice or watch the gold flakes dance around the hazel pools of her eyes.

"Spots and I need to step out for a few hours. Just finish off and lock up when you leave. We'll see you on Monday."

"Oh, okay." Her face dropped and I left not looking back.

I know girls, I know women, and I know facial expressions and body language. Mia wanted me just as much as I wanted her. I could see it in the way her face lifted every time I walked in the door, how she sucked in tiny puffs of air every time we accidentally touched, how her skin prickled and her body tensed. I knew it because my body did the same. But I wasn't going to let either of us get sucked into the spiral of desire. She was off limits and so was I.

I was almost at the door when she tried again. "Where are you going?"

"Out." I closed it behind me wincing at my own callousness. I shrugged it off. Survival is a cold bitch.

"Come on buddy, let's go see Simone. She misses you, boy." I patted Spots on the head as he jumped up, tail wagging.

I held the door open for Spots, and my eyes flicked over to the office. She was sitting on the chair with her head down. Her tight skirt hugged her thighs, showing off a bit of flesh beneath. Her fuck-me boots swung to some unheard music, and she bit her lip, her forehead creased. She looked delectable. She shifted in the chair and her head spun, her eyes finding mine. My heart thumped in my chest as if I had just been caught stealing the collection money.

She didn't smile, but I wanted her to. So desperately. Her gaze was penetrating, probing, and bewitching. I pried my eyes away from hers and walked out, letting the door slam behind me.

———

I was knee-deep in dog shit and dog food when my cell phone rang, vibrating gently in my pocket. I pushed Spots away as he licked my hand, and I reached for the phone. It was the office number.

"What's wrong?"

"There's…um…someone here…" Mia stammered on the other side of the line. An icy chill ran down my back and the hair on my nape rose. Images of Rita flashed in my mind as my hand tightened around the phone.

"She says she knows you."

"She?" She. My heart calmed a little, and I could swallow again. "Who is it? Are you okay?" I heard mumbling and clinking in the background.

"She said her name is Alice."

"Fuck."

Fuck.

Fuck.

Alice.

I guess it was inevitable; one day she would fall down the rabbit hole again, come around sniffing and fuck it all up.

"Do not let her in the office, and do not let her in my room. Keep her in the kitchen and away from everything sharp. I'll be right there."

I could hear Mia's voice calling to me down the phone, but I was already hanging up and heading out the door.

I kissed Simone on the cheek, "Sorry, it's Alice."

She gave me a sad smile, "You never have to apologise, Gabe. You do more here than you really need to."

I nodded and called for Spots. "I don't think I could ever really do enough."

Simone put a tentative hand on my shoulder, "It's not all your fault, Gabriel."

"Isn't it?" My body felt heavy and wracked with guilt, but I had no time for any of that just then. I had to get to Mia. To Alice.

We were sprinting back to the workshop the minute my feet hit the pavement outside of the shelter. Spots trying to keep up, his limp causing him to fall behind. The lump in my throat tightened.

I burst through the heavy iron door and stormed through the workshop, meandering around the cars that sat on the floor.

"Mia?" I called out.

"We're here." Her voice sounded frantic.

I found Mia standing by Alice, who was slouched like a rag over a plastic chair. Mia's clothes were covered in vomit and the stench filled the small room. Alice's eyes were fluttering, and she mumbled incoherently to herself.

"How long ago did she vomit?" I sidestepped Mia and reached for Alice, pushing her into the seat, trying to keep her body upright. It was like trying to thread a needle during a hurricane.

"Maybe two minutes." Mia's voice was calmer now, but her eyes were wide and wild.

"Alice? Alice, can you hear me?" She didn't respond, her eyes closing, her body like water flowing off the chair and onto the floor in a puddle.

Her shallow breathing was the only sign she was still alive.

I turned to Mia, "Call an ambulance, tell them she's OD'd. Probably heroin."

Mia nodded and took my phone from my hand, her voice turned to a murmur as she spoke far away. I studied Alice's face. She wasn't doing well. The colour she had gained drained from her features like leaking paint, and her fuller body suddenly seemed empty. Her scarred arms showed signs of her stupidity. Why the hell was she using again? She was doing so well.

Her chest rose and fell with barely audible breaths.

"Shit."

I scrambled to my feet and ran to the cupboards searching for the first aid kit. I yanked the black handle and sprinted back, throwing it down by Alice's head. The hard, metal box clanked violently against the concrete. I rifled through the contents discarding Band-Aids, gauze, bandages and ointments.

I found the Evzio at the bottom of the case, and my fingers curled around it. When it became available on the market, I bought one but always hoped I would never have to use it. I guess I was a realist. I fucking hated Alice for making me have to buy one, for predicting this day would come.

I grabbed the Evzio and stabbed it into Alice with force. It probably wasn't necessary, but it almost felt good to deliver the Naloxone so brutally.

Alice sucked in a deep breath and moaned.

Mia returned to my side, "The ambulance should arrive shortly."

"Okay, thanks." I wanted her to go, to leave. I didn't want her to see Alice like this, but I also didn't want her to see me like this—vulnerable, weak, helpless.

Sweat broke across Alice's forehead, and she began to shake.

"Should I get her a blanket?"

"Not yet."

"But, she's shaking."

"I know, just wait."

Sirens wailed in the distance, and I hoped they were for Alice; the meds would last for at least thirty minutes, but she might need a second dose. I glared at the empty needle in my hand, my fist closing around it. I should have bought a second dose.

I could see the change in Alice's face, her skin pulling, and lips tightening. The convulsions were coming. I turned to Mia. "Grab a bucket or something. Hurry!"

Mia placed the bucket by Alice's face just as it pulled back. I lifted her head and she lurched into a heaving fit, spewing what was left of her last meal.

She groaned again and opened her eyes. They focused for a second and she smiled. "Hey kiddo, I came to see you." Her smile was a mask of horror smeared across her face.

"Why, Alice?"

"I have something for you."

"That's not what I meant." I pinched the bridge of my nose, my eyes slamming shut.

"Sorry baby, it's just that..." her words fell away and she shrugged as if that was enough explanation.

The sirens drew closer, the noise leaked through the rolling door, red and blue lights flickered from the windows, coating the white walls. A thundering knock hammered through the room.

"I'll go let them in." Mia left the room.

"Alice..."

Alice lifted a bruised hand, reaching for my face. I flinched away from her touch.

"Hey, don't be like that," Her smile was twisted and bent. "I came to see you."

"Hey there." A male voice boomed in the room behind me. I turned to see a man dressed in navy paramedic coveralls, a large bag slung across his shoulders.

I stood up and studied the man. He gave me a sad smile. I knew he was being empathetic; but all I saw there was pity, and all I wanted to do was slap it off his face.

"Her name is Alice Notte, forty-nine years old. I'm guessing heroin. She had a dose of Naloxone about seventeen minutes ago. There's been vomit and shallow breathing."

The paramedic's eyes grew darker and sadder. I stepped out of his way, knowing I had done all I could. He bent down and spoke to Alice. She smiled at him. A second man walked in. He seemed out of place. His pretty face twisted as he smelled the stench of vomit and lifted as he eyed Mia. I clenched my fists at my sides as the older paramedic got his attention.

"Hey Phil, help me out here. We are going to take Alice here to Silver Crest hospital." He gave Alice a warm smile. "She needs a place to rest for a while and someone to watch over her.

Phil pried his eyes away from Mia and bent down to help pick up Alice. She looked like a feather, thin and flimsy and ready to float away. She certainly didn't need two men to hold her up or carry her.

When she was upright, the two paramedics lead her to the waiting ambulance outside. "Will one of you be joining us?" The older of the two asked before they left the room.

I just shook my head. My jaw clenched.

The paramedic tipped his head as Alice sagged in their arms.

"Wait," She groaned as they led her out of the room, "Happy birthday, kiddo." It fell like lead into the silent room. I heard Mia's soft gasp and could feel the pity as it leached from the two men carrying my mother away.

When the door slammed behind them, Mia stood in the centre of the room, leaning against a plastic chair as if it afforded her some sort of protection from the mess she'd just witnessed. Her eyes searched my face for answers I didn't want to share.

"You need to get cleaned up."

"I'm okay." She crinkled her nose at the vomit soaking her singlet, it stuck to her body like stinking glue

"Follow me."

"Who is she?"

"Don't worry about it."

Mia hadn't budged from her place by the chair. Her wondering eyes, full of questions, burrowed themselves into me, searching for answers I didn't want to give. "Is she your mother?"

"She's Alice."

"Gabriel?"

I sighed rubbing my hands down my face. "Yes."

In a few strides, she was next to me, a delicate hand lifting my chin, her eyes full of concern were searching mine. "Are you okay?"

Was I okay?

Why did the question beat against me like a hammer

threatening to shatter all my walls? Why did her concern pierce so deep that it was like a stab? Why was she asking? I wanted to scream, to fall to my knees, to break down and weep for the childhood I never had, for the dread I've carried waiting for the phone to ring, waiting for a corpse to identify.

No, I wasn't okay; I wasn't anywhere near okay. But her delicate hand on my chin, the sweet caress of her fingers soothed the pain just a little.

"I'm fine." I lied; because the lie was always easier than the truth.

I peeled her hand from my face and laced my fingers through hers. "Come on."

She allowed me to lead her to my room and stood waiting as I searched my cupboard. I pulled out an old T-shirt, the one I wore the night I was with Rita. It was going to be too big, but it would have to do.

"You can use my shower." I handed her the shirt and a clean towel, "This is clean. You can wear it when you go."

"Thank you." She bit her lower lip and headed to the bathroom.

I crumpled onto my bed, my head cupped in my hands. The pipes hissed and screeched to life, and steam leaked from the semi-open door. My eyes shifted to the gap. Through the opening, I glimpsed movement. My body stiffened and I sat up. Mia's image appeared in the mirror.

She tore off the ruined singlet, and her purple bra clung to her body as she tugged at her skirt. With dainty, practised moves, she unclasped her bra and released her breasts. I sucked in a deep breath and felt myself harden. Her perky nipples danced in creamy pools of swollen flesh. They would fit into my hands perfectly. My mouth grew wet as she took her underwear off. There she was, naked and glorious. All I wanted was to break that door down and bury myself inside her, to find release, relief. I almost felt guilty.

Almost.

My cock twitched and pushed against my jeans. Mia stepped away into the waiting shower, and her figure disappeared as the mirror fogged over.

I imagined her in the shower. My shower. Lathering soap on her body, washing my mother's sick off her skin. The thought gave me the slap I needed. I lay back down, breathing and sucking down all the savage thoughts that consumed me.

When the pipes died down, my body stiffened once more. I lay still, waiting and forcing my eyes on the ceiling, knowing that if I saw her again I would have no will power to hold myself back. I would have to take her.

Claim her.

Make her mine.

And then, I would break her.

When the door opened, she was wrapped in a towel. Water droplets clung to her flushed skin. I could understand why, once I touched that smooth skin, it was too hard to keep away, to not hold on to it forever. I needed it. Hair stuck to her forehead in wet clumps, and her face bore none of her makeup. Her usually bright-red lips were pink and soft—and just as delectable. Her pile of clothes hung in her palm, her bra like a cherry on a mismatched cupcake.

"I'll give you some privacy."

I bolted from the bed and slammed the bathroom door behind me. I needed distance, I needed to wash the day away. I was still covered in dog shit, hair, and slobber; and now, Alice's vomit and disgust. I needed to wash away the desire, the pain, the lust, and anger.

My mind was in shreds as I stepped into the steaming shower. Despite the scrubbing and churning, I didn't feel clean; I didn't feel relief.

I dried off and wrapped the towel around my hips. When I opened the door, my heart leapt to my throat.

"What are you still doing here?" I wanted to sound cold and angry, but I was too tired; too tired to fight my desires.

Mia's eyes grew wide as they took a leisurely journey up my body. My dick twitched in response. I've seen that look before—appreciation, desire, heat.

Mia rose from the bed, my T-shirt looking far too big on her slim frame. She had slipped back into her skirt and boots, and her hair cascaded in damp waves along her neck.

With a few long strides, Mia closed the distance between us, stopping only inches away.

I was suddenly very aware of being naked below my towel.

"I wanted to make sure you were all right."

Fuck. Why did she have to be so soft? So caring?

"I've already told you I was fine." I brushed away her concern, but she didn't move.

She raised her hands to my shoulders, my stomach coiled at the touch. Ever so slowly, she traced the slope of my muscled arm and trailed across to my abdomen, her fingers light and delicate, sending hot shivers across my body. She curled her index finger in the hairline just below my belly button. She yanked at the hair lightly, eliciting a low hiss from me. She pulled through the trail coming to a stop at the boundary of my towel. My breathing became ragged, and my heart drummed an uneven beat.

She lifted her eyes to mine. I could see myself there, wild hair and narrow eyes, want and desire spilling everywhere.

Mia trailed her fingers back up and wrapped two hands around my neck, pressing herself against me. I sucked in a deep breath as we both felt my body react. My cock twitched, swelled, and grew.

"What are you doing?" My voice was scratched and hoarse.

"No one should celebrate their birthday alone."

Before I could speak, her lips were on mine. I had a split second to think, to react.

I stood motionless as her lips beat against mine, frozen and unresponsive. I allowed her to humiliate herself against me as my body raged, and my soul shattered.

When she pulled away, her face was twisted and her eyes glittered with tears. Her lips quivered as she studied my face; hers full of questions, and anger, and pity.

God damn pity.

"It's not my birthday." My voice was back to its frigid temperature.

Nail in the coffin.

Her hand cracked across my face, leaving behind a hot sting. Mia turned around without another word and ran out of the door. Seconds later, I heard the iron door slam. It echoed my heart, chugging against my chest.

I pounded at the wall. My fist clipped the door frame, and skin scrapped off my knuckle leaving a long red smear.

"Fuck!" I yelled at the wall, at the emptiness, at my pain.

It was my thirty-second birthday.

—⚔—

I expected Salvatore to call me at sunrise saying he'd had no luck, but it took less than three hours for my phone to ring. The searing heat of my anger and frustration flamed as I hung up the phone. Nothing seemed to work that night. Not a single fucking thing could take the edge off; not jerking off or running with Spots, not even downing a few shots.

Every time I thought I might be over the cauldron of feeling that bubbled inside me, I would think of Alice's blue lips and Mia's glossy red ones, Alice's shut eyes and Mia's teary ones, Alice's hoarse voice and Mia's husky, needy one. I couldn't get them out of my head. The cauldron kept bubbling as they cast their spell on me.

So, when Salvatore called, I focused on my goal. I had one mission. My head was finally clear.

I marched to the storeroom and grabbed a roll of large plastic sheets. The plastic clung to my sweaty arms as I made my way to the back of the workshop.

I had rearranged a lot of Tony's mess, and that included a lot of renovations; but, as I've said before, he was not a stupid man and if I hadn't learned from him, I would have been dead already. Like Tony, I also had a back room. The kind that only a few people in the world knew about. It was a third of the size of Tony's, but I didn't need much space to beat a man to death.

Oh, did you still think I was a good guy? You need to be paying better attention.

I felt for the hidden panel and pushed the button which in turn popped. A door slid away from the fake wall, allowing me access into the room. I waited for the door to shut completely before I switched the lights on. The fluorescent lights exploded to life with a dull buzz. I set the sheet on the floor and placed a single chair in the middle of the room.

I texted Salvatore that I was in the back, and he assured me he was five minutes away.

I switched the lights off and edged along the wall to the opposite side of the room. Waiting.

Darkness amplifies everything. Fear. Desperation. Loneliness. Anger. My thoughts burned into me in deep, painful furrows. Insanity was a dark, deep rabbit hole.

I heard the latch of the door and straightened up. The sound of pathetic whimpers filled the small space and was soon followed by the crunch of plastic sheets as Salvatore and his man walked into the room.

"Lights, boss."

I covered my eyes and could feel the light as it burst to life beyond my eyelids.

When I opened them, Salvatore and Joe were strapping in their cargo. I studied the snivelling mess that now occupied the chair. His clothes were dishevelled and hung off his body as if they were waiting for him to grow into them. His thinning brown hair was peppered with white, tumbling well below his shoulders. Blood and snot dripped from his nose and stained his long moustache and beard.

He looked at me through scared, blue eyes which darted from me to his bound hands.

I remained silent assessing this man. His story could have been sadder than Alice's, but I didn't give a fuck. I wondered how many kids he had fucked up in his wake? How many lives he had ruined with his choices? It didn't matter. That night would be the last time he did any of that.

"There's been some kind of mistake." He finally started snivelling.

"Salvatore over there doesn't make mistakes." I kept my voice calm and even.

"Look, I don't know what you think I did, but I mean you no harm man. Just let me go, I have no debts to anyone."

"You do now."

"No, man, no. I'm all paid up." He clenched his fists and, for the first time, I noticed he was missing a little finger from both hands as well as the ring finger on his right hand.

"No, you're not."

The man shook his head, and his fingers twitched and moved as if he was counting. He mumbled to himself then finally looked up. "I'm all paid up."

"Do you know Alice?"

"Everyone knows Alice." For a second he forgot his predicament and relaxed. I knew why. He was thinking about Alice. But not like I was. He was thinking about her sucking his cock, or wrapped around him, or bent over a park bench.

I grimaced at the answer and he flinched, his head hitting the back of the chair.

"What's your name?"

"Fat Rob."

My eyebrow arched by itself. "I used to be a bigger man." He gave me a weak smile, a gaping hole in his gums where his teeth should have been.

"Did you see Alice tonight, Rob?"

"I did, for a minute."

"Just a minute?"

"Maybe more."

"Tell me about it."

He swallowed and smacked his lips together then pulled on the restraints. When they didn't budge, he started. "I was begging on the intersection of Oak and Fir. There's always good traffic there around morning time; you know all the fancy people going to their fancy jobs in their fancy sui—"

"I don't give a fuck about them, Rob." It was a harsh whisper that sank all the way to the pit of his stomach. I saw it in the way his eyes shifted and body recoiled. I've seen that look on many men before. "Just tell me about Alice."

Sweat broke on his forehead and he nodded. "She walked past me. I didn't even recognise her at first, you know. She looked amazing. All filled up and clean. You know she has hips now you can really hold on t—"

My fist connected with his cheek and his head flayed backwards, smashing into the back of the chair.

He screamed in agony and tried to fight the restraints. I know the feeling of stinging pain that you can't do anything about; all you have to do is feel it, let it sink in and burn. Accept that it won't go away and move on.

"Alice." I hissed

Rob cried and snorted in loose snot. He shook his head

and continued through sobs. "She recognised me, man. I didn't even..." He sucked in a long breath, trying to calm himself. "She offered me a hot meal. You know how long it's been since I've eaten anything hot and in the presence of..." He flinched as I moved, "A lady?" He finished and I let it be.

"She bought me a hot soup. I told her I had no way to repay her, and she said she didn't need any money; she had someone looking after her, and that she could help her friends and such now a little bit."

"Rob." I stopped him and he baulked at the mention of his name. His eyes, wide and rheumy, flickered wildly across the room. "Just tell me how Alice got high today."

At that, he froze. His neck pulled back and down like a toddler, thinking I couldn't see him if he stopped looking at me.

"Rob? Has the cat got your tongue? Just a minute ago you were telling me about soup."

Rob shook his head mumbling to himself.

I threw my body weight into the next punch; my patience was running thin, and my frustration had gotten the better of me. I drew my hand back and ploughed it into his stomach. I could see his face collapse as all the air expelled from his lungs. His howl was pained and broken as he sucked in small breaths, trying to regain relief. His hands and legs fought the restraints. But before he had the chance to recover I punched him a second time, this time across the eye. I heard the mild crunch, and his flesh turned an angry red. I knew it would start to swell in minutes.

His body sagged as he snivelled and cried, fighting the pain, fighting the anguish, fighting his hopelessness.

"Last time Rob. Alice. Where did she get the drugs?"

"I…I…I…I…offered her some."

"She's been clean for two years, why would she take it from you?"

"She wanted it."

"Did she?"

"Hey man. It's the truth. Alice used to be a good-time kinda girl." He winced at my growl. "The Alice that was next to me, she looked great but she wasn't the Alice I knew. She was bone dry and boring, and she wasn't really livin', you know?"

"*Livin'*?" I cocked a brow, my voice hissed at the man who shrivelled against the hard chair.

"Yeah man, you know, You gotta live if you wanna be alive."

I clenched my teeth and, suddenly, all I wanted was another shower.

"So, what happened?"

"I told her she forgot who she was, and I offered her a quick hit. She said no. So, when she wasn't looking, I slipped some into her coffee. You know, just a taste. A reminder. She mellowed out real quick after that."

My fists shook and my jaw hurt from the tension.

"I told her I had more where that came from and showed her my rocks and powder. I took her by the hand, and she followed me to the park. Willingly. She wanted to come. I cooked her up a batch. I smoked a few rocks and that was that."

"That was that?"

"I…I…I…Yes, that was that."

"Rob. I'm going to ask you just one final time. That was that?"

"Well…" I stood up and he flinched as my body stalked his pathetic shape. "She let me inject her and then she kind of laid there, you know? All happy and content and beautiful. I just couldn't help myself, and she never said no. She started vomiting about half way, twitching and convulsing and shit." His face twisted as mine darkened. That motherfucker was going to have a very bad night. "Anyway, when she started getting sick, I brought her here. You know, this is the place. Everyone knows her son lives here. Or used to. She told everyone about him. All proud and shit. Anyway, I have my own problems man. So, I left her. She seemed a little better. She was talking and standing. I left her with a woman. She seemed okay."

"She seemed okay?"

"She was talking…standing…" he swallowed. "She was coming here anyway, something about a birthday…" He hung his head and pulled on the restraints once more.

"How many times did she say no?"

Rob leered at me through cracked lips, "Come on man. You know Alice never says no to—" The sound of his head smashing against the back of the chair as my hand connected with his jaw was satisfying.

I bent down by the chair so he would have to look at my face, so there was nowhere else to look. "I was talking about the drugs. How many times did she say no?"

"I don't know man." He grunted an airless sound as my fist connected with his belly. I could almost feel his spine as my hand moved through him.

"How many?"

Rob cried and snivelled, his body trying to cave in on itself. "Maybe five, maybe more. I wasn't counting, man; I was just trying to give her what she wanted."

I stood in silence, contemplating his words.

"Thank you, Rob, for being honest with me."

"No problem, man." His mouth turned in a hesitant smile. "Look, just let me go okay? I'll go smoke a bit and, by morning, I won't even remember what happened. I'll think I got mugged again or fell down the subway stairs."

I chuckled at his optimism.

"Now Rob, I think that I'm going to give you what you want."

"Really?" His smile lightened across his broken face.

"Thanks, man. I really thought…" He fell silent as Salvatore walked forward with a needle.

"Hold him down."

Salvatore and Joe walked over to the chair and grabbed Rob. Salvatore pinned his shoulders to the back of the chair while Joe grabbed his wrists, immobilising him completely. Helpless. He tried to fight, but a sack of bones was no match against two heavy-set men who have known physical violence since birth.

I approached Rob. "Look at me."

His rabbit eyes darted across the room still searching for a way out. "Alice was clean, you asshole. She's been clean for two years, and tonight she almost died because you needed to stick your cock in something with a pulse."

"No—no it's not like that." Salvatore clamped a hand over his mouth. Rob's neck corded with tension.

"Real life things, as you call your conversations, should really involve the people's lives that your choices fuck up. The choices you make and the consequences. Today, you made a choice to stick your dick in my mother, and the only way you could do that was to get her back in the fucking gutter with you. Cause, you're a filthy rat."

He tried to talk against Salvatore's hand, but all that emanated were muffled sounds.

"I wanted your way out to be painful but, unfortunately, I have so little time. And, quite frankly, you're a piece of shit and I don't want to waste any of it on you."

I tied a short piece of plastic tube around his arm and slapped the skin, waiting for his collapsing veins to pop up. Rob screamed; his tears glistened on Salvatore's hand. His legs pushed and strained against the leg restraints.

The needle sank softly into his flesh and, in a matter of seconds, Rob's body sagged and his eyes glazed over. Salvatore and Joe released their hold on him.

"How do you feel, Rob?" I cooed.

"Mmmm it's so good, man." His slack face beamed. I continued to pump more into his veins, tripling the dose any addict could handle.

His body became slack, and he sagged deeper into the chair, his face lolling, his eyes heavy. "How does it feel, Rob?"

"They made me...she didn't say..."

"Rob? What are you talking about? Who made you?" I slapped him across the face.

He didn't respond. I suspect he couldn't. Not with the amount of heroin I had just pumped into his body. His eyes shut and his breathing became shallow.

He lost consciousness.

Fuck. If someone sent him to hurt Alice, it was too late to ask. I used my only shot of Naloxone on Alice. There was no saving Fat Rob.

"Fuck." The anger ignited inside me once more, and my fist took it out on Rob's lolling face.

Salvatore and Joe returned to their positions by the door. Silent sentinels of death, they awaited their next instruction.

We waited. Rob's face paled; a peppering of clammy sweat covered his forehead, and his lips were tinged in blue. His body didn't fight long. His breathing became more erratic, gurgling and choking on itself.

I looked at Salvatore. "Make sure they don't find him too soon. And see if you can find out more about anyone trying to hurt Alice."

Salvatore nodded and walked over to the chair where he undid Rob's restraints. Rob slid like jelly from the chair as if his bones had completely evaporated.

I walked out of the room and into the workshop. My anger had evaporated and all that was left was exhaustion.

The only gifts I got for my birthday were a broken heart, an overdosing mother, and a corpse.

Someone should put that on a T-shirt.

PART VII

She barely looked at me. For weeks. Nothing but cold stares and clipped conversations. Mia avoided me at all costs, and it broke me time and time again. Like a wave against my wall, she pounded and crashed, but I had to stay strong—for both of us. Letting her in would mean danger for both of us. That's not something I could do to her.

Thoughts of her filtered through my every waking moment—the brief taste of her lips on mine, the smell of her skin, her pink nipples and rounded ass, my shirt swaying on her skin. She was perfect. Even angry, she was stunning. Glaring eyes and snarling teeth, like an animal.

So when she didn't show up on a Tuesday morning, her absence was searing. Nothing felt right, as if somehow an integral cog in the system snapped off and the machine was breaking down. The phone didn't stop ringing, and nothing seemed to flow, jobs weren't getting done, even a simple oil change ran into problems. The machine needed its cog.

I strode to Mia's office. It had ceased to be mine the day she walked into my workshop. I picked up the receiver and dialled her house number.

"Hello?" Her voice sounded hoarse and gruff.

"Where are you?"

The silence stretched for a minute till it was broken by a coughing fit.

"I'm sick." her response clipped and agitated.

"When will you be back?"

"When I'm better." She fell into another coughing fit and hung up the call, the receiver going dead in my ear.

I marched downstairs and barked at Joe. He was in charge until I got back. He tipped his head and went back to work. I snatched the keys to my '67 Camaro.

I drove, my foot heavy on the accelerator and my jaw clenched. My knuckles turned white as I weaved around cars and tore through traffic. Who did she think she was? Hanging up on me? And why the hell didn't she let me know she was sick? How sick was she? Was she coming back?

My heart flared with fear and worry. Damn, it was too late. She had somehow crawled under my skin, and now there was another person I felt responsible for, someone I wanted to look after, someone I cared for. I tried to so hard to keep up the walls, but she found a crack and she beat me.

I pulled up outside her apartment and pounded on the door.

When no one came to open the door, my pounding grew more insistent, louder and angrier.

I heard the chain on the door, and my fist fell to my side. Mia opened the door just a crack, her puffy eyes grew wider when she saw me.

"What are you doing here?"

"Spots was worried about you."

"Spots?"

"Yes."

"Where is he?"

I pushed the door open and let myself in.

She sneered at me and walked away, falling onto her couch covered by a mountain of blankets. Mia climbed beneath them and clawed the blankets over her shoulders. Used tissues lay in piles around her like a flurry of snow.

Her usually bright eyes were sunken and blotched. They seemed heavy as her head compressed into the pillow.

"Why are you here?" She whispered, her eyelids growing heavy.

"Just sleep, Mia. Everything will be okay."

I wasn't even sure if she heard me. Her tiny body rose and fell beneath the blankets.

As she slept, I looked around at the small apartment. A single bedroom that she had transformed into her own private castle. Despite the walls being grey with age and peeling at the corners, she filled rooms with greenery and bright colours. Next to her neatly made bed was a side table covered in books and two framed pictures of horses. The first horse had a glossy chestnut coat, with big round eyes that followed me around the room. The other, was a bay coloured mare, alert, with stocky limbs. I guessed that would be Jigsaw.

I returned to the tiny lounge. The two-seater sofa, that was now occupied by Mia, took most of the space. A small TV was tucked in the corner of the room, and a small table leaned against the couch, holding the box of tissues and an empty glass of water.

She looked so fragile laying in a curled ball under all those blankets. Her limp hair covering her clammy face. What she needed was rest, and I was going to make sure she got it.

On my left was a kitchen that contained a standard white fridge and stove with a few cupboards hanging above a workbench. An empty bowl was set in the drying rack. It reminded me of so many nights alone, my heart panged.

I approached the couch and kneeled beside it, tucking my hands under Mia's body and lifting her easily from the couch. With eyes still closed, she murmured and nuzzled her face into my collarbone while wrapping her hands around my neck. It was the place I wanted her to stay forever. I laid her on the bed, watching as her body unfolded and stretched out while I piled her blankets on her.

I returned to the lounge, cleaned up the avalanche of tissues and went to check what she had in her kitchen.

Nothing.

Not exactly nothing—if you count a half-eaten loaf of bread, some jam, three packs of two-minute soup, and a banana that was more black than yellow.

I sighed and raked a hand through my hair.

I searched the apartment till I found her key. It was hooked inside a cupboard, tied with a green ribbon. I let myself out, returning an hour later with some food and medicine. I emptied the food into the fridge and stole back into her bedroom. Mia had barely moved since I placed her on the bed. I smoothed her hair away and placed a hand on her forehead, it sizzled. She was burning up.

I slipped off my shoes and jacket and sank onto the bed beside her, leaning against the backboard.

She moaned and turned, her heavy eyelids fluttering open. I could see confusion cloud her eyes as recognition set it. She didn't quite sit up but jerked beneath the blankets.

"How did I get here? What are you doing here?"

"You seemed uncomfortable on the couch." She just stared at me as if she couldn't comprehend my words. "How are you feeling?"

"Cold. Really, really cold." She pulled at her blankets, and I reached over placing my hand over her forehead again. "You're burning up. Here, I got you something to help with that." I grabbed the paper bag with the paracetamol, popped out one of the pills from its plastic sheet and handed her a glass of water.

She gulped the entire glass.

"Good, you need to keep your fluid intake up."

"What are you, a doctor?"

"Just a concerned employer."

"So, you do this with all your employees? Break into their houses and lie on their beds uninvited?"

"No. But maybe I should start."

Her mouth curved in a half smile and it occurred to me how beautiful she was, even with grey-skinned and cracked lips. Like a wilted flower, but a flower nonetheless.

"What are you doing here, Gabriel?"

I shrugged.

How could I possibly explain that I couldn't keep away from her, despite all my attempts? How could I tell her that all I wanted was to have her in my arms and make her mine? How could I tell her that if I did all those things, I would break her?

Her raspy voice pierced through the heavy veil of my thoughts. "Gabriel?"

"Get some rest." There was no fight left in her, her tired body already drifting off. I watched her eyes flutter and her forehead break into a sweat. I watched her hair grasp at the moisture and clump against her skull. I watched her dry lips twitch with dreams. I tried to memorise every moment and every inch of her, trying to preserve them in a perfect memory that I could keep with me forever.

At about three am, she jolted awake. Light leaked from the kitchen. Her damp hair was pasted around her face. I rolled my hand over her forehead, and she gasped, then froze.

"Shh, it's me," The back of my hand brushed her clammy skin. "Your fever has broken."

"You're here? I thought I was dreaming"

"A good dream then?" My eyebrow arched.

"Why are you here?" She moved away from my touch.

"I couldn't leave."

"Couldn't or wouldn't?"

She reeked of day-old sweat. Her black singlet clung to every curve and crevice, and droplets of sweat hung between the swells of her breasts.

"You need a change of clothes; you're soaking and you smell."

"You need to stop all this." She folded her arms across her chest.

"Come on." I rolled off the bed and walked around to her side, extending an arm out to her. She turned to face the window.

"I'm fine."

I bit my top lip and inhaled deeply. "Either you get up and shower or I will pick you up and shower you. One way or another, this is going to happen."

"Gabriel." She brushed me aside, looking away.

"Three."

Her head whirled around, and she met my gaze for the first time. "What the fu—"

"Two."

"Okay. Okay." I offered my hand as she lifted herself from the bed. She sidestepped me and walked to her bathroom, slamming the door behind her. Moments later the pipes churned and coughed to life. I lifted the blankets from the bed to reveal an almost human-shaped puddle.

I pulled the sheet off her bed and searched through the main cupboard till I found a clean sheet. I wrapped her bed up and unfurled the blankets. The pipes had died down, and suddenly I was left alone in the shadowed room with my heart pounding in my chest.

The door opened and a burst of cloudy steam poured out, followed by Mia. She looked half human, draped in a towel.

Her eyes flicked to her bed and to the pile of sheets on the floor. "Did you change my sheets?"

"How do you feel?"

"Better, but I feel the cold coming back." Her teeth clashed together.

"You better get dressed." I walked over and took her hand, leading her to the bed. That time she didn't resist. "Where do you keep your pyjamas?"

"You didn't look through all my stuff?"

"No." Her face almost fell. Did I disappoint her? Did she want me to riffle and dig up all her skeletons? Was I a fool not to?

"Now, where do you keep them?"

"Gabriel I can dress myself."

"Where?"

"Top right drawer." She didn't fight, she was still weak. If she was better, she would have fought me tooth and nail. In fact, despite my brushing off her questions, I would likely have been kicked out hours ago.

"Underwear?"

"On the left."

I stuck my hand into the left-hand drawer and blindly fished out the first pair I grabbed. I did the same with the T-shirt and walked over to the bed kneeling at Mia's feet. A position I had dreamt of taking since the first time I saw that gap between her boots and her thighs.

I guided her legs into the holes and pulled up the fabric, my finger brushing her smooth skin as it journeyed up and disappeared beyond the towel. Fighting every primitive urge that clawed at me, I turned my head away allowing her privacy to adjust.

Mia sat back down, and I pulled the shirt over her head. Once her hands were inside the sleeves, she released the towel.

"Here, have this." I popped out two more pills and handed them to her with a glass of water. She sucked at the liquid greedily. Her lips latching around the glass. Everything about her screamed at me. I shook my head trying to dislodge the thoughts.

She lay down, and I layered the blankets back on top of her. I rounded the bed and sat opposite her, studying her face. Her gaze latched onto mine.

"What?'

"Why are you here, Gabriel? What are you doing here?"

"I'm just making sure you're alright."

"But why? You obviously don't want me. So, what do you want?" Her brow creased and her mouth pouted.

I plunged my fingers into my hair, her anguish leaching the strength from my body. I won. I made her believe it. I needed to her to believe it. I was free. I should have been elated, relieved; I should have told her she was right and walked out of that room and out of her life. Yet somehow, my hand found its way to her jaw and traced the soft skin. "I do. Since the moment I saw you."

"Don't say that…"

"Mia—"

"And when I am better, you'll go back to scowling and frowning and avoiding me." Her mouth turned down at the corners and tugged at my heart like small anchors.

"Tell me about Cookie and Jigsaw; tell me about your farm, your family, anything. Why are you here? Why did you need the job so much?" What I really wanted to ask was why she had to walk into my calculated, perfectly-planned life and ruin everything just by being her, by showing up and smelling so damn good, by dressing like a school girl who cut her skirts too high and wore her shirts too tight—and those fucking boots. I needed something before I suffocated under the weight of desire and the need to have her, to destroy her.

"Why do you care?"

"I need to know who I have working for me."

She huffed. "Need to know?" She turned her back to me.

"Yes." I clenched my jaw. I was losing her, maybe I had lost her already.

"They've both been turned to glue, if you really want to know." Moisture pooled in her eyes. I clenched my fist, resisting the urge to kiss away her tears.

"Who?"

"The horses." There was a quiver in her voice. "There, now you know. Are you happy?" She craned her neck and her face was full of challenge. Twisted and tortured, marred by raw pain. Pain that I caused.

"No Mia, seeing you like this doesn't make me happy at all." My chest ached with the weight of her pain, and I wanted to take it all away. I raked my hands through my hair again and sucked in a deep breath.

I lay down stretching my body along hers and winged an arm around her. She stiffened for a second. I waited. When she said nothing, I pulled her close against me. Her heat searing me.

"No, Mia, mia luce," I repeated planting a single soft kiss at the base of her neck. "I never want to make you sad."

"What does that mean?"

"My light. You are the light in all the darkness Mia."

"I didn't know you spoke Italian."

"I don't," I graze my teeth up her long neck. "When I was a kid, Alice put this old black and white film on the TV. She sat with me and hugged me through the whole thing. At one point the main character said those words to the woman. Alice told me what it meant. It stuck with me. Maybe because it's the only thing she really taught me." I shrugged at my words.

"Gabriel." she sighed my name as if resigned.

I pulled her closer still, as her body softened and moulded against mine. My mind flooded with need; a need that had nothing to do with the deviant desires I had towards her, but all to do with the feelings I was pretending I didn't have for her.

Her breathing became shallower and her chest fell and rose against mine. I enjoyed her softness against all my hard edges, the feel of how her body fit perfectly around mind. Having her this close made my body burn.

"Oh, luce mia," I whispered over her. "You're driving me crazy."

I fell into an uneasy sleep, fighting the demons of my desire.

—

When I woke up, she wasn't in the bed. Light filtered in from the rest of the apartment that somehow seemed lighter, as if the oppression of sickness had lifted, like a demon has been exorcised. I remained motionless, listening. I could hear faint clinking and a soft pop. A moment later, the smell of fresh coffee filled the room. I sucked it in letting it wash over me. I just had the best sleep I've had in almost ten years. I felt like shit.

I got up and went straight to the bathroom. I splashed water over my face and gurgled some water and toothpaste. When I re-entered her room, I made the bed, opened the curtain, and cracked the window open to allow the air to freshen it.

She froze for a second when she saw me in the door frame, her face relaxed and she looked at me from under long lashes as she took a long sip from her coffee. She hadn't put on any pants, and my eyes flicked over to her long, slim legs drowning under the oversized T-shirt.

"Are you going to offer me one of those?" I grizzled.

"Figured you must know your way around here pretty well, so you can just help yourself."

I raised an eyebrow and cocked my head. She just

shrugged, sidestepped me and went to sit on her couch. She folded her legs beneath her and sat facing me, her face taut with the effort of not smiling.

"How do you feel?'

"Good. I feel fine, thank you."

"Good." I searched for my shoes. They were by the door where I left them. My jacket hung over the side of her couch. I grabbed it and slipped it on.

"You're going?"

"No one is making me coffee." I shrugged.

"Gabriel I—"

"I need to get home to Spots. He doesn't like being alone."

"Oh, right." She tapped a finger on her cup, the gentle tinkle the only sound between us. "Gabriel?" Her hazel eyes were full of wonder, creased at the corners with hesitation. "Did you mean what you said last night?"

"Which part?"

"That you don't want to make me sad."

I bit the inside of my lip, where was she going with this? "Yes." I slipped into my shoes avoiding her eyes.

"Well then, can you stop avoiding me at work? Can you stop pretending there's nothing between us?"

I slammed my eyes shut. When I opened them, I looked right at her. "No Mia, I can't do that."

"Why?" Her jaw clenched and her back straightened.

"Because there is nothing going on, and there never will be."

"That's bullshit and you know it."

"No."

"Lair."

I took a step towards her, my nose flaring, "Don't call me that."

"Then stop being a fucking coward and tell me the truth. Why did you stay here? Why did you take care of me? And why do you avoid me all the time?"

"I already answered all those questions." I took another step until I was looming over her shape on the couch.

"With lies." Her neck corded and her teeth bared, and all I wanted was to tear her clothes off and fuck her like the animal I was.

I bent over her, my face inches from hers. My hand found her neck, and my thumb rested on her chin. "Because, Mia, I am infatuated with you. You're too beautiful and too smart and too fucking sexy. You've invaded my dreams and my life, and you've crawled under my skin. I cannot stop thinking about you; your red lips and your soft skin, your smart mouth and your incredible smile." My hand squeezed around her, "But I cannot have you, I do not want you, and I will not allow this to happen."

Her eyes blazed and she flicked her tongue over her lips. "Liar." She hissed.

My mouth slammed into hers, and my fingers dug into her flesh as she kissed me. Her tongue slipped past my lips; coffee and mint danced in my mouth as her hands closed around my face, and her fingers tugged at my hair. My heart thundered and the air crackled around us. She moaned and it was all I could do to not be completely undone.

I pulled away and met the challenge in her eyes. Wild and needy, desire painted her body.

"It's too dangerous." I stepped back and reached for the door, slamming it behind me. I heard her call my name, just once. I didn't stay. If she opened that door or called me again, I would not have been able to stop myself, to walk away from her. My whole body was on fire, lit by lust and desire, by the need to own her and break her, feel her and claim her.

I should have fired her, should have pushed her out of my life, should have fucked her and dumped her and never given it a second thought.

Except that I would have.

I would've never been able to wash her scent off me; the

feel of her would forever echo on my body and burn beneath my skin.

I needed her.

I wanted her.

She had to go.

———

She took the rest of the week off, which both pissed me off and scared me. It pissed me off, cause I knew she was fine. But it scared me, because I wondered if I was ever going to see her again, taste her again, feel her again.

Mia walked in the following Monday morning dressed in a buttoned-up shirt. The top three buttons were undone, the collar pulled wide to reveal the swells of her breasts and the cups of her black bra. She tucked it into a short skirt that hugged her body and highlighted all her curves.

She strolled right by me without a sideways glance and slammed the door to her office, where she stayed for the remainder of the day. When she was done, she walked out. She spent the entire day pretending I didn't exist.

Good.

Not good.

Perfect.

For the rest of that week, she continued her little game. Each day she dressed more provocatively than the next. She made no eye contact, even as I struggled to peel my eyes away from her. She didn't address me in any way, didn't come down to the workshop, and didn't say goodnight at the end of each shift.

By Thursday, I was eating myself up from the inside. She was only doing what she was told.

But was she?

On Friday afternoon, Mia strolled onto the workshop floor and said she needed me to look over some paperwork with her. She found a discrepancy and couldn't work it out. She tried to remain calm, but her voice was somewhere between anger and despair. We were both hanging in the same tree, stretched out on parallel limbs; the only question was whose would break first.

My heart thudded against my chest as I approached her. Accounting papers spread over the desk. I inhaled her scent. The manufactured wildflowers mingled with her earthy tones of rich grass and open fields. It was intoxicating being so close to her again. The faint odorous reminders she left behind every day were no match.

"How's Alice?" Her tone was formal and cold.

"Fine."

"Good. I'm sorry about what happened, I never meant t—"

I cut her off, "Did you bring me up here to talk about my mother?"

"No."

I leaned over the desk, my elbow brushed her arm, and she flinched away. My insides constricted with heartache. I clenched my jaw and sucked in a deep breath.

"What's the problem?"

"This." She pointed to a line of print she had highlighted and pointed to a number of other pages that spanned the last decade.

I glanced over the pages knowing what they were. "That's not a discrepancy."

"But these transfers have no name and don't follow logical patterns. Random figures, random dates, same account. The amounts seem too big."

"They're not too big."

"Are you hiding money somewhere?" Her eyes blazed with accusation.

"No." I remained calm despite the venom in her voice.

"So, what are these?"

"Donations."

Her face crumpled in disappointment, and she reached for her bag. "You know I need this job, but I will not get involved in anything illegal."

I didn't move. "There's nothing illegal going on here."

"Then tell me what these payments are for." She turned to look at me, her eyes wild, her face heated, and her mouth slightly opened—just enough to slip my tongue into.

"You'll just have to trust me. All those are above board."

"Trust you?" She laughed and made to walk by me. I turned my body and blocked her path. She tried to sidestep me, but I stepped in her way again.

"Trust me." I searched her face. I could see the battle behind her eyes, it was raging inside me also; the body and the brain at war, wrong and right, good and bad, darkness and light.

"I can't."

"Why? When have I given you a reason not to trust me?"

She stepped back and laughed again. The laughter held no mirth, just desperation. She folded her arms across herself and flayed me with a look. "You're a liar."

I ground my teeth and inhaled, "I told you not to call me that."

"And I told you, I can't be involved in anything illegal."

"Fuck Mia, what do you want? The money is donated."

"To who? You don't have a charitable bone in your body, and none of these so-called donations are claimed back on your tax."

"It's because I don't want to claim it back."

"I don't understand."

"Because you're not meant to." I sighed and pinched the bridge of my nose.

"Move out of my way." She pushed against me, and suddenly I was wracked with the need to prove to her that I wasn't such an asshole.

I grabbed her arm and said, "Let's go."

"Where?" She pulled against me, resisting, fighting.

"You wouldn't believe me if I told you. So I'll show you."

The tightness in her face softened, and she allowed me to lead her out of the room.

I released her arm at the top of the stairs and called Spots. "Hey boy. Hey buddy. Do you want to go visit Simone?" I noticed the tinging around Mia's mouth when I mentioned the name and smiled. "She misses you a lot. Let's go see her." Spots leapt up and I scratched his head. His tongue lolled and he jumped to the door, leaping up and down in anticipation.

I held the door open for Mia and she squeezed by me, her body avoiding mine at all costs. I smirked and followed Spots who was already several meters ahead.

We walked in a charged silence. Angry electricity crackled between us—mistrust and loathing.

"Why are we walking?" Mia grumbled after a while.

"I like walking."

"How much further?"

"Not much." I clenched my jaw, holding back a smile. "Don't you like spending time with me?"

Mia huffed and increased her pace, following Spots who was leaping up and down. His twisted leg scraped at the pavement.

We rounded the corner, and Spots bolted in through a back door. It was cracked open and the backlight shone in invitation.

Mia gave me a questioning look, and I nodded. But she stopped by the door unsure.

A whiff of wet dogs and dry dog food coated the air as I opened the door and stepped inside. The narrow corridor was lined with shelves stocked with dog food, blankets and shampoo. I made a mental note that Simone seemed short on flea powder.

I gestured for Mia to follow. Through the door, we could hear the barking and howling.

We followed the light till we walked into an open space. Eight pens lined the walls and housed a number of dogs. Simone stood in the middle of the room, Spots jumping up and down while she ruffled his head and scratched his ears.

When we stepped into the room, she looked up and her face lit up. "Hi, Gabriel. I wasn't expecting you today."

"I wasn't planning on coming, but Spots missed you."

"Of course, he did." Her smile widened. Simone rounded her desk and pulled out a treat.

"Here you go, Spots. You're just a good boy."

Spots grabbed the bone and went to perch on a dog pillow by one of the pens. He chewed idly, his tail wagging wildly.

"And who is this?" Simone noticed Mia for the first time. She stood in the middle of the room, her eyes wide, her mouth slightly parted, and her hands limp by her side.

"Sorry, Simone. This is Mia." Comprehension crinkled her already furrowed forehead, and her eyes twinkled.

"Oh! So you're Mia."

Mia's head cocked as she heard her name. Pulling her shoulders back and holding her head high, she was all business. She extended her hand out to Simone, who raised a questioning eyebrow at me. I shrugged. Simone accepted the hand and shook it lightly.

"You know about me?"

"Your name has been mentioned once or twice." Simone knew politics.

"Ah." Mia let the subject drop with Simone's hand. "You're a dog shelter?"

"Yes. Thanks to Gabriel and his generosity, we've managed to become one of the biggest in town. We also offer some veterinary services."

"How many dogs can you house?"

"At any given time, we house between thirty and fifty dogs. Our capacity allows for seventy but, I'm happy to say, it's never come to that." Simone gave Mia a warm smile. "Come, let me show you."

Mia flashed me a look as Simone grabbed her hand and pulled her away. Simone was about to give her the grand tour. The nursery for the sick and the injured, the playroom, the introduction room—Simone was in her element, the crow's feet around her eyes softened, and the lines around her mouth stretched out as she talked about the place and animals that she loved.

I watched Mia.

Arm in arm with the older woman, she allowed herself to be whisked away by the excitement; she showed genuine interest and made Simone feel heard, loved, respected. That was the one thing she was incredible at—making you forget all your faults, making you feel like you were the most important person in the room at just that one moment. I could see how Simone took to her.

Every now and again, Mia's eyes flicked over to me. Something akin to confusion and appreciation clouded her face.

When they returned, Mia was hanging on Simone's arm as if they had known each other for years. They giggled and clutched and snorted. It should have felt incredible. Somehow, it felt invasive. As if this woman had invaded my private sanctuary. She has already taken over my office and had been in my room more times than an employee ever should. Now she was here at Paw Prints Rescue, hanging off Simone, falling for her charm and her stories, indulging in her caring nature, and the face that put you at ease and never judged—not ever.

I wanted to hold on to these rueful feelings, to dwell in spite and anger. But hope churned in my guts. Hope that Mia saw me as something other than a dark hole, an all-consuming piece of shit. Hope that she could, if only momentarily, believe that deep down inside I wasn't a monster.

But you know that isn't true, now don't you?

Simone led Mia back over to the corner where I had slid against the wall and was patting Spots. Oblivious, he chewed on his treat. Both women looked at me and their faces lit up. It was as if Simone's admiration had infected Mia. Her cold and callous demeanour seemed to have melted away and was replaced with something akin to forgiveness.

Simone released Mia and stepped over to me. She bent on her haunches and patted Spots, who released his treat and licked her hand. She giggled at his enthusiasms. "Oh Spots, you're a good boy, Yeah, you are." She scrunched her face, spoke through pouted lips and planted a kiss on the top of his head.

Simone's forest green eyes locked with mine, the crows feet stretched under a smile. "I see what you mean." She whispered to me and returned her attention to Spots. I pushed away from the wall and stood up.

"We can't stay. I still have work to do. I'll be back on Saturday. I see you're running out of flea bath; send me a list of anything else you need."

"Why don't you take the weekend off? I have Alex coming for a few hours, and she's much better with people than you are."

I shrugged, no point arguing facts. "Sure. But, I still want that list."

"Of course." She looked to Mia, "I don't know what we would do without our guardian angel."

Heat rose to my ears. I raked a hand through my hair and tried to push the embarrassment down. Why did I feel like a kid around this woman? Why did I care what she thought?

Mia shot me a lingering look, "I bet."

"Come on buddy, home time." Spots skulked up, the treat still half eaten in his mouth.

"Why don't you leave him here with me again? He can have a play with some of the other dogs, and he'll stay upstairs with me like last time."

I looked from Simone to Spots and back to Simone who beamed at me.

"He'll be fine. You know he will."

I sighed. "Hey buddy, do you want to stay the night?" Spots let his treat drop to the floor and leapt up at me, licking and wagging his tail. "Okay buddy, no problem." He rubbed his nose against my hip once more then jumped down, retrieved his bone, and returned to the corner bed.

"I guess he's staying."

"Great, it'll be nice to have some company."

"I'll come pick him up tomorrow."

"Sunday will be fine too." Simone winked at me and turned away towards a large bin containing dog food. "I have to do dinners and water, so I'll see you Sunday." She shot Mia a quick look, "Nice meeting you, Mia."

"You too, Simone."

I led the way down the narrow hallway and waited for Mia to exit, before I made sure I locked the back-entry way.

I shoved my hands into my pockets and started walking, Mia silent by my side.

"Why didn't you just tell me?'

"Would you have believed me if I did?" I stopped and looked at her, my shape looming over her.

"No." She averted her eyes.

"I know what you think of me—"

"You have no idea what I think of you." She cut me off.

"I'm sure I could guess." I stopped dead and turned towards her, my body pushing her against the building. "You think I am some kind of broken bird with clipped wings.

And that if I just let you in, that you could mend everything that's broken."

"You give yourself too much credit." She huffed at me.

I raised an eyebrow.

"Yes, you've had some issues. But you're anything but broken. You're strong. You are so fucking strong that you're a fort; you've built walls so high around yourself that you can't even see what's on the other side. You want to be cold, but you're anything but. You're like a volcano; there's so much heat and warmth brewing inside you, it just wants to spill out. But you keep it all inside, dormant. Only a select few ever get to see the splendour of an explosion."

I swallowed hard, my heart racing. I took another step, and my body pinned hers against the wall. Heat rose from somewhere inside me, submerging everything.

"You are dangerous—I can see that—but you're also a protector. You protect those you care about, and you protect your heart so fucking fiercely. Because deep down, despite all your strength and passion and danger, you're are afraid just like the rest of us. You're afraid of getting hurt and losing yourself and actually showing people who you are."

My mouth slammed into hers, even as she was still unravelling me. Her soft lips parted and her tongue darted out to meet mine. My arms closed around her, pulling her against me, my hips grinding against her. She moaned into my mouth, sending me reeling.

My hand travelled up her back and plunged into her hair; I gathered a handful in my fist and tugged, forcing her face upwards, deepening the kiss. Her body writhed against mine. I broke away from her mouth and peppered kisses along her chin, travelling the length of her long neck—naked, flushed skin. She moaned as I kissed her collarbone, the scent of her intoxicating.

I found her mouth once more, hungry, wet, devouring. All the while, my erection ground against her, my hardness pushing against my jeans, wanting to taste her, wanting to have her, wanting to fuck her.

I needed her.

I wanted her.

I wasn't going to deny myself any longer.

It would all be so easy. I could've just pulled up her skirt, tore away her underwear, released myself from my jeans, and I'd be undone.

But I didn't want it to be easy.

I didn't want it to be quick.

I wanted to revere her, devour her, claim her, and that took time.

I pulled away from Mia. She was flushed and breathless and totally breathtaking. "Not here." The words scratched through my voice as I grabbed Mia's wrist and pulled her behind me. I took long purposeful strides; I would have sprinted if not for her shorter legs and the rigidness between mine.

I pushed through the red door as if it wasn't even there. I yanked Mia through it, spun her around, and slammed her body against it—shutting it with a loud bang. My lips found hers.

Needy.

Desperate.

Hungry.

So very, very hungry.

"Mia." I growled as I pulled away tugging at her bottom lip.

My hands found her waist, and I lifted her up. She wrapped her legs around my hips as I pinned her to the door. Our eyes locked, our breath erratic. Our lips sought each other and, once again, we were one. Her hands raked through my hair, fingers digging into my scalp, scratching at my neck.

With her body pinned against the door, and her arms

winged around me, my hands were free to explore her. I tugged at her shirt releasing it from the skirt. One by one, I unbuttoned her shirt, exposing her flesh and her black lacy bra. I groaned at the sight of her.

The shirt hung off her shoulders as my hand travelled along her silky back, rounded her ribs and found the swell of her breasts. I cupped the right one in my hand, wanting nothing more than to rip her bra off and have her skin in my hand.

But I waited.

I found her nipple as it rose and hardened behind the material. My thumb rolled across the growing bud, and I pinched it. She moaned, pushing her hips against mine, burying her head into my neck, nipping at my skin. I did the same on the other side, craving her skin, punishing me, punishing her.

I buried my hand in her hair and tugged at the strands, exposing her neck to me. I peppered kissed along it, grazing her delicate skin, tasting her, wanting more of her—all of her.

I grabbed the strap of her bra in my mouth and edged it off her left shoulder. Her hard nipple peeked at me beneath the rim of the fabric. I hissed sucking in a long breath. My cock twitched and pushed in eagerness. I pulled off the other strap, her nipples danced as she ground herself against me. I kissed her collarbone and the swell of her breasts, my tongue lashing at her nipples—so pink, so hard, so perfect. Her whimpers sank deep into my core, drawing from me a fierce ache for more.

So.

Much.

More.

Mia pulled, then yanked until she wrenched my shirt from my body. Her eyes roamed my torso. Her fingernails dug into my neck and she pulled me in, her legs squeezing around my hips, her need burning. She exhaled into my mouth with a soft eager moan as my hands tightened around her.

I pulled at her skirt, lifting it like a band around her ass, and my hand slid underneath, finding the elastic of her underwear. My fingers slid beyond the lace and brushed along her hot, wet lips. She moaned and trembled, the sound sparking lust and greed in my already needy body. The weight of desire too much to hold

I retrieved my hand and hooked myself around her. I pushed away from the door and walked to my room. No more games, no more denial, only Mia.

I lay her on my bed and stood beside it appreciating her beauty. Her hair, tousled and messy, framed her heated face. Her blazing eyes darting over me. She licked her glistening lips, red and swollen. She peeled the white shirt from her body, exposing creamy soft flesh. Her skirt, pushed up along her legs, revealed their endless expanse.

I unbuttoned my jeans and pulled them off giving my cock breathing room. I prowled onto the bed and blanketed her with my body. Finding her lips, I kissed her. Not urgent, like I wanted. Not hungry, like I was. But sweet and soft, like she deserved. She answered with her own need.

I broke away from her mouth. My fingers traced the shape of her jaw and journeyed down towards her neck where they closed. Pushing against the jaw bone, I forced her head back, her body arching for me. With my free hand, I pulled away her bra. I groaned at the sight of her breasts. My hand travelled freely between them—twisting, pinching, stroking, kneading—and when she shivered and moaned, my mouth found reprieve on her skin. I wrapped my tongue around her nipple, my teeth grazing the hardened bud. Her soft gasps and trembling body were maddening.

"Gabriel." She moaned my name, and I almost unravelled

right then. The reverence in her voice, like a knife in my heart, threatening to shatter the solid ice around it.

I released her and pulled myself away. With one fluid movement, I unzipped her skirt, tore it away from her body, and relieved her of her underwear. I exhaled at her beauty, the rounded shape of her hips, the dark curly hair at the apex of her legs, her flat abdomen.

All of her.

Was mine.

My fingers and tongue teased, brushing and grazing around her as she moaned and quivered.

"Please." She begged. So I obliged, continuing to touch her, all her hidden curves, every inch of skin, every unexplored depth.

Kissing.

Teasing.

Sucking.

Brushing.

Stroking.

Wanting.

"Gabriel, please." She trembled. Her body, peppered in sweat and heated with desire, was breaking for me.

I unwrenched myself from her quivering body and threw off my boxers. I grabbed a condom from my drawer and rolled it on, returning to the only place I wanted to be.

Crawling back onto the bed, I pushed her legs apart and lowered my mouth to her opening. She moaned at my hot breath. My cock responded to the sound, swelling, hardening, needing.

I plunged a finger into her, and she groaned bucking her hips. Clasping her hips, I held her down and my tongue flicked over her. Her sex, musky and sweet, was like a drug I could get addicted to. Completely intoxicating as I devoured her, slow and measured. I tortured her, whipping her with my tongue. Lashing. Striking. Punishing.

Holding her down, fighting the grinding of her hips along my face, I watched the beautiful grimace of delight as her face creased and her chest rose and fell in a frenzy. I dined on her like she was my last meal.

She was close, so close and I wanted her to suffer, just like me, to ride the wave, to fall and crash together.

I left her a quivering mess—desperate, hungry, needy—and climbed above her. My cock at her entrance, the heat already sending me into a frenzy. I wouldn't last long.

With a desperate groan, I plunged inside her and all my walls collapsed. My eyes latched onto hers as I moved inside her, her hips pushing against mine, opening, tightening, trembling. I answered her need, pumping faster, needing more of her, all of her; I couldn't get deep enough. I wanted to crawl under her skin and become part of her. Nothing was enough.

Harder.

Faster.

Tighter.

She trembled beneath me—soft, sharp moans drowning me and pulling me under.

I was so close. My heart raced and my vision clouded as Mia arched herself into me. With a long, searing cry, she clutched at my back—her fingernails tearing at my skin—and tightened and convulsed around me.

With a few languishing thrusts, I sank deeper into her. And with an anguished delighted groan, I came undone. Pleasure crashed into me in a wave of voracious sensation, shuddering against her soft flesh, smashing against her sweaty skin and heavy breaths.

I collapsed on her. My entire weight sinking into her hot and sweaty body, her heart thumping through me, her breath hot at my neck.

Bliss.

When my body settled, I rolled away and, instinctively,

she curled herself into me. I held her. Unintentionally. Desperately. What the hell did we just do?

I kissed her shoulder and she mumbled something, her body pushing further against mine. I wanted to drown in her —the soft swells of her chest as they rose and fell against me, the waves of her wild hair as it stuck to her back, the musk of her sex, the beads of her sweat, the feel of her softness. And so I did; I closed my eyes and drowned.

⸻

"*G*abriel. Gabriel, wake up." *Her voice was so distant it felt like she was part of my dream. "Wake up, Gabriel. We're going to go get some ice cream."*

My lids felt heavy as I strained to open them. I was still so tired. The room was pitch black. I shut my eyes again.

"Come on, kiddo, we're going to go get some ice cream." Light flashed behind my eyelids, and she shook me insistently.

I opened my eyes and stared at Alice. "You look like a princess." I smiled at her. And she did. She had on her favourite gold shirt that sparkled in the light, a small black skirt, high heels and a long, beaded necklace. She had makeup on and was smiling. That happy smile, the smile I loved. And we were going on an adventure—in the middle of the night.

"Hurry up, kiddo." She pushed me from the bed. I rolled off the mattress and pulled on my pants and winter Jacket. I found my beanie by the door. Alice grabbed my hand and yanked me down the stairs and into the cold night. The cold air stung my face. I already missed my bed. But Alice was back.

She hadn't been back for two nights. Sometimes, even when Alice was home, she just stayed asleep. But tonight happy Alice was here again, and she wanted to take me on an adventure.

"What flavour ice cream would you like, kiddo?"

"Isn't it too cold for ice cream?"

"Who told you that?"

"You did. A couple of days ago."

"Na, it's never too cold for ice cream." I beamed at her.

Alice rambled on as we walked, promising adventures and excitement. I skipped next to her as she trotted ahead, her heels clacking on the dark pavement.

The takeaway was open twenty-four hours. The lights blazed in every direction. In the dark night, it spilt on the road and surrounding business, bathing them in an orange glow that felt almost warm.

I told Alice I wanted a strawberry, chocolate cone. So I complained and my eyes welled with tears when she shelled out a few coins for a plain vanilla ice cream.

"Look kiddo, you got an ice cream. Now, stop complaining."

I swallowed my tears and licked the ice cream, following my mother. Her steps growing faster, her body vibrating with excitement.

"Ok kiddo, we're just going to go meet a friend, okay? You just eat your ice cream."

I nodded and followed her to a tall brick building—just another building in a stack of endless brick monstrosities. She pressed the doorbell and the front door buzzed allowing us access to the building.

We took the elevator and stopped on the seventh floor. Alice knocked on door 709. She flipped her hair and flashed me a smile. "How do I look, kiddo?"

"Beautiful." She flashed me another smile as the door flew open. A man opened the door. He was big and hairy, and his mouth cracked open in a smile when he saw Alice.

"Hey, gorgeous." He grabbed her and kissed her on the mouth. My stomach coiled when he touched her. Something didn't feel right.

His eyes landed on me, and he looked at Alice again, "What the fuck is he doing here?"

"I couldn't get anyone to watch him. He'll be fine, he'll just watch TV or something. You won't even know he's here."

"Just keep him out of the way."

"No problem, Danny." She smiled at him but his frown didn't go away. He watched me as I followed my mom inside. Danny closed the door behind us and wrapped his hand across my mom's shoulders. "Entertainment is here boys."

We walked into a lounge room where a bunch of other men sat, they all cheered when they saw my mom. My heart swelled with pride; she had so many friends that loved her.

There was another girl there, but she looked tired, her eyelids were heavy. It was really late.

"Okay kiddo, you sit here." Alice pushed me onto the couch next to the girl, a trail of drool was crawling from her mouth and pooled on the couch. She murmured as my body shifted her weight. "Don't move. Just stay here and when I finish with my friends, we will go home."

I nodded and licked the ice cream; it was melting into my hands. There was an old action movie on the TV. I watched the cops chasing some bad guys out of town.

I don't know if I fell asleep or if I was just so engrossed in the movie when I noticed I was alone in the room. The girl had vanished and so had all the men. I hadn't seen Alice since we arrived. My hand was sticky with dried ice cream. I got up and wiped the exhaustion from my eyes. I needed to wash my hands, and I wanted to sleep. Alice's play date was taking too long.

I heard the noise. It was coming from a room. The door was cracked open. I stepped closer. There was a bed. The sleeping girl was on it now. It looked like she was still sleeping, but all her clothes were gone and one of the men from before was lying on top of her. He was grunting and pushing her with his body. She wasn't waking up.

I pushed the door open and found Alice. Her clothes were also gone. Everyone's clothes were gone. She was bent over the bed, and there was a man behind her. He was pushing into her from the back and grunting like a pig every time his hips slapped against her ass. His forehead was peppered with sweat and beads of it shone on his long beard. The other man knelt on the bed in front of Alice, and he had his thing in her mouth; but it was bigger and harder than mine had ever been. He had her hair in his fist, and he was pushing her head up and down. A third man was watching. He was touching his thing too; it was up and hard, and he stroked it up and down. And then his eyes fell on me.

"What the fuck?"

It was as if time stood still. Everyone froze for a split second, and all eyes in the room landed on me. Except for the girl that didn't want to wake up. I saw my mom's face. It was wet and sweaty, her hair messy and her mascara smudged in long black lines down her face. Was she crying?

"Get him the fuck out of here, Steve."

The man who was touching himself took three strides and was in front of me. He grabbed the collar of my jacket and yanked me away from the door.

I could hear Alice shouting something, and one of the other men told her to 'shut up and suck.' I didn't want to go with this man. I didn't want to leave my mother there. But he was bigger and stronger, and my jacket was zipped right up to my chin. He opened the front door and pushed me outside.

"Just stay here, kid. Your mom will be fine." He slammed the door in my face, even as I banged against it. I banged and banged, pounding the door with my fists, pushing against it, slapping with a flat hand when my knuckles got too sore. When my throat was raw from screaming, and my hands throbbed in pain, I sank to the floor. The corridor was dirty and dim and smelt like piss. Noises filtered from beyond cardboard walls and thin doors.

I tried to sleep; but every sound and bang woke me and left me shivering and more petrified than before. Mommy would come soon, she's going to come soon, I'll be home soon, I'll be home soon. I chanted the mantra over and over, clutching my knees and wiping hot tears from my cold face.

Sun filtered through the small hallway window when I woke up again. She hadn't come out yet. My stomach growled. I sat waiting.

People came in and out of doors. Big, small, dark, pale, tired and bothered—they all had that same look of desperation. That look people get when they give up fighting, when they just give in to the fact that this is their lot and nothing would ever change.

I kept waiting. Minutes, hours, maybe days. The sun had moved slowly, and my stomach growled more fiercely with each inch. I waited.

The door cracked open and one of the men from the night before stepped out, almost tripping over me. "Watch your step, kid!" He roared at me and walked towards the elevator. When he had gone, I tried the knob. The door gave way and opened.

I stood listening. There was silence. I walked into the house. One of the men was asleep on the couch, his body slopped like a rag over the stained, grey fabric. I tiptoed around him. The kitchen was deserted. The room where my mother had been was now occupied by the sleeping girl. She was still there and still naked, two of the men were asleep on either side of her.

I found Alice in the second bedroom. Danny was wrapped around her; they were both naked and asleep.

I sat by the side of the bed and waited for Alice to wake up.

***

The dream was too real. Sweat drenched my face as my eyes flew open. I sucked in a deep breath and looked around. I was in my bed with Mia. With Mia.

I looked at the shape of her, curled and splendid as she slept. As quietly as I could, I rolled out of the bed, found my boxers and slipped them on. I needed a drink. Leaving the room, I made my way to the office. The pale night drenched the workshop and office in a grey light. But I knew my way around the place and didn't need more light.

At the drinks cart, I grabbed a tumbler and tossed some ice into it. The cubes clinked in the glass and splintered with a hiss as I poured the vodka over them. I sipped the drink, savouring the burn down my throat and the spreading warmth in my chest.

I was on my second glass when her shape appeared at the door. Her long, silky silhouette clad in an oversized shirt with endless legs, wavy wild hair and naked feet.

"Are you ok?" Her voice was laced with concern.

"You should be sleeping." My voice strained at the sight of her.

"I was. Then I woke up to a cold, empty bed." She stepped into the room.

"Bad dream."

"Want to talk about it?"

"No."

She came further into the room and leaned against the desk. In the pale light her skin shone almost blue and her hair a glittering grey.

"Would you like a drink?"

"No. How many have you had?"

"Just the two. I'm considering a third." I swished the near empty glass and brought it to my mouth, sucking the last of the drops of alcohol.

"Tell me about your dream."

I glanced at her, "I said I don't want to talk about it." I sank further into the seat. Mia's face grew grim. With two long measured strides, she closed the distance between us and mounted me. Her hands slinking around my neck as her legs hooked behind the chair. A shiver ran up my spine at her touch.

She lowered herself to me, seeking out my lips. Soft and tender, her kiss was gentle and exquisite.

"I can't make it better if you don't tell me." Her hips begun a slow dance against my groin, and my cock responded immediately.

"Mia," I groaned her name, lost in delicious agony. "I said I don't want to ta—" Her lips sucked at mine again, her tongue sweeping by them. She deepened the kiss, raw and brutal as she used herself as a balm.

"Poor, broken Gabriel." Her hips rolled above me in an undulating motion, her fingers brushed my jaw, the bristles rolling beneath her touch.

"Mia." My hands clutched the chair beneath me, my knuckles white.

"It's okay, Gabriel. Just let go. Let me make it better." Her hands plunged into my hair, and her lips brushed mine then pressed forcefully—needy—her tongue gliding past my lips. She sank into the kiss—into me—and I was hers.

My knuckles brushed the inside of her thigh, and she shivered at my touch, grinding gently against me.

My hand travelled beneath her shirt, finding hot flesh. I clutched her hips, digging my fingers into her. I wanted her to stop. And needed her to keep going. She rolled against me, with me. My fingers brushed the length of her, finding their way to her breasts. My thumb brushed over a nipple, so perfectly erect that she arched her back, pressing into my touch with a soft moan.

"Mia," I whispered into her. I was hard and swollen and unravelling fast. "I don't want to pretend anymore. I want you." My voice was guttural and breathy.

"You have me." She pressed herself lower onto me, and a shy smile stretched across her lips.

"No, not just this. I want more of you, all of you." I hissed as she ground against me, her mouth falling open. "You keep me up all night, and you haunt my thoughts each day. I've wanted you from the moment you walked in and every minute after that."

There was so much more I wanted to say but Mia pulled away. Her heat leaving mine, the sensation almost painful, the disconnection unbearable. She reached over to the desk, pulled open the bottom drawer where she rummaged around, and pulled out a foil package. Her hands found the elastic of my boxers, and she tugged as I lifted myself off the chair. Her fingers swept the length of my cock, and I jerked at her touch. A smile tugged at her lips. and she handed me the small foil square.

I rolled the condom over my erection while Mia pulled the shirt from her body. It was all I could do to hold on. Her perky breasts danced with her movements, her nipples tight as pinpricks. She slid out of her underwear and, in a beautiful fluid movement, was back in my lap.

"Let me make it better." She whispered in my ear as she positioned my cock at her entrance and sank onto me. I growled at her tight heat, and my fingers curved around her ass, clutching onto the flesh.

"I feel so powerless with you; everything is out of control. I can't protect you, can't stop the pain."

"What pain? What are you talking about?" Her brow furrowed as her hips rolled up and down. I hissed at her heat.

"If anything happened to you…"

"Just. Let. Go, Gabriel."

Her hips moved above me, willing me to bury myself deep inside her. Her hot flesh searing mine. My hands trailed her spine and raked through her hair, exposing her long neck. I nipped at the flesh, biting, licking, and sucking. Her groans were like a siren call, her body moving above me in a sensual dance. I trailed the path to her breast and sunk my teeth into the swollen flesh, swirling my tongue around her pink nipples, drawing soft ,desperate moans from her. Her back arched and her fingernails dug into my shoulders. She looked tortured with happiness, her face contorted. I could have been hurting her or giving her immense pleasure, they looked one and the same with her face like that. I didn't want to stop; I couldn't even if I tried.

Pulling her into my mouth, I held her with one hand while the other found her wetness. I swallowed her soft moans as they grew louder, each belonging to me, forcing her body to shiver, drawing from her pleasure so divine that she exploded all around me. Her hips pushing, pulling, burying, as my hands tightened around her. My hips bucked and drove into her in a mad frenzy until, with a final desperate stab, pleasure coiled in my core and erupted in waves of lust and desire.

Breathless, we both gulped erratic breaths, and she settled her forehead against mine. Our gazes locked. She dropped her mouth to mine and drew a soft moan from my lips as she kissed me so delicately—as if she could feel how fragile I was.

She climbed off me, her body glistened with sweat while mine already ached at the memory of her touch.

Mia reached for her discarded shirt and slipped it over her head. "Get rid of that thing and come to bed. I don't want to sleep alone."

She turned around and walked out of the room without a backwards glance.

I clenched my jaw at the wake of her silence, got up and discarded the condom in the wastebasket. I grabbed my boxers and walked downstairs.

In the dim light, I could make out her figure under the blanket. I slid beside her, curling around her body, wrapping my arms around her, her heat a comfort. I gathered her hair in my hand and pushed it away, exposing the delicate spot of flesh where her neck and shoulder met. I planted a single kiss and she murmured, pushing herself against me, allowing me to gather her into me—closer, hotter, desperate.

"Mia..."

"In the morning Gabriel, I don't want it to end yet."

I didn't argue. How could I when I felt the same? I fought sleep. Sleep brought nightmares and brought the sunrise. Sleep would steal her away from me—her smell, the feel of her around me, the soft rise and fall of her chest, the curve of her body. I fought. And I lost.

I swallowed the pain in my chest as I bolted up in bed. The dream had returned. It was always the same, and always different. This time the end felt so real and so close, too close. I grabbed my chest, willing to quell the pounding of my heart that screamed in agony. I sucked in deep, long breaths. The room became clearer, the light of day forming shapes in my bedroom, reeling time forward.

"Is that how you always wake up?" Her voice was a mixture of concern and curiosity. My eyes shot up and met hers.

She was sitting cross-legged on a chair she had dragged over to the side of the bed. She was watching me sleep.

"How long have you been awake?"

"Long enough to avoid another smack to the head."

"Sorry." My eyes flickered over her face. "Did I hurt you?" I clenched my fists under the blanket, wanting to tear the mattress to shreds.

"Not enough to scare me away just yet." A shadow of a smile flickered on her face, and the softness of it allowed some of the tension to seep from my body.

I shoved myself to the edge of the bed when she shot me a sharp look. Her eyes studied me with piercing scrutiny. "Don't move."

I stilled. Waiting.

"We're going to play a game."

"Oh?"

"It's called truth." Her eyes remained fixed on me, gauging any reaction. When I gave her none she continued, "I ask a question, if you answer truthfully, you get a reward."

"What sort of reward?" My body jerked at the ideas spilling into my head.

"You can ask me to touch you or touch myself, in any way you see fit."

I swallowed hard and my cock jerked to life, suddenly hard and eager. I sucked in a deep breath, trying to remain calm.

"What sorts of questions?"

"Easy ones. Hard ones."

"And do I get to ask any?"

"Maybe."

"I'm not sure your game is fair."

"Life's not fair. Are you ready?"

"No."

"Question one. Is Alice your mother?"

"Really?"

"Answer the question, Gabriel."

"Yes."

"Good. Now, claim your reward."

"Kiss me, Mia."

A wicked smile spread across her face, and the tip of her tongue slipped out of her mouth licking the top lip. God, she was so sensual. She slunk like a cat onto the bed, her hand and knees sinking into the sheet that clung to my body. The sheet tugged at my bare flesh and sent goosebumps along my spine. She brought her mouth but a hairsbreadth away from mine. Then swung away and planted a hot kiss onto my chest.

I grumbled. Turned on, and disappointed all at once. "That wasn't what I meant."

"Then you should have been more specific." She winked at me and I scoffed.

This game was going to hurt.

Everywhere.

She retreated back onto the chair, her legs curled beneath her. "Question two."

"Isn't it my turn to ask a question?"

"Not yet."

"I'm not sure I like your rules." I ground my teeth and waited.

She ignored my complaint. "Why do you live here?"

I sighed and my eyes swept the room, cramped, dark, completely safe, and comfortable. All too familiar. "It's the only place I can call home." Her dark eyes scrutinised my face, looking for traces of lies, hesitation. Or maybe she was wanting more. There wasn't going to be any more.

"What's your reward?"

"Take off that shirt." My voice scratched, low and gritty.

Mia uncurled her legs, and her arms crossed herself as she reached for the hem of the shirt. She pulled it up ever so slowly. My eyes feasted on her body as, inch by agonising inch, she bared herself to me, exposing her naked creamy torso, followed by her breasts that bounded and fell with the motion of her arms, her puckered pink nipples, and her long neck. When she released her head from the shirt, her wild brown hair fell in waves framing her flushed face and covering the swell of her breasts.

I groaned at the sight of her, my body hardening. My fists dug into the sheet, stretching the fabric to its limits, the soft cotton rubbing against my erection. Threatening. Comforting. Arousing.

I would not survive this game.

The T-shirt landed mutely on the floor as the last strands slipped off her arm. Mia crossed her legs again, not trying to cover up her nudity, not shying away from the task she had set herself. My mouth watered at the sight of her.

"Question three." She ran her fingers across her lips. "Do you have a second set of books for this place."

"No." It wasn't a lie, but it wasn't the truth either.

"No?'

"Every penny I make and earn and pay out is all clean. This place," I breathed—my home, the home built on a pile of lies and bodies—"It's as clean and pure as I can fucking make it." I didn't bother hiding the bitterness that tainted my voice. I couldn't be angry at her for the accusation and yet, I was. She didn't trust me. Not yet. And after today, after this game of hers, I didn't know if there would be any winners or if we would both lose.

She nodded as if accepting my answer despite her reservations of whether or not I was telling the truth. That was the olive branch she was willing to extend, and I would grab onto it with both hands.

"I want you to touch yourself." My voice was cracking at the seams.

Mia bit her lower lip and raised a hand to her mouth where she sucked the tip of her finger. She popped it out, her lip curling below as her finger fell to her chin and traced the long curve of her neck.

My body hardened as my eyes glued themselves to the tip of her index finger which was now tracing an agonisingly slow path from the hollow of her neck, down between her breasts, to the lining of her black underwear. Her finger lingered, and in a painstakingly deliberate move, retraced its original route, sinking back into her mouth with a soft moan.

I gulped for air as my breath stalled, my lungs feverishly trying to keep up with my heart, my pulse hammering, pounding, rocketing. She was playing with me like I was a toy, and I was completely captivated by her game.

"Question four." Mia sat back on the chair and gathered her loose hair, twirling it around her wrist. The motion forced her back to arch while her breasts danced and moved with her.

"No."

"No?" She let her hair drop and edged forward on her seat.

"My turn." I tried to sound forceful, but I could hear the despair in my voice. I was begging. I needed a reprieve.

Her hand shot back to her hair, and she twirled a long, brown strand around her finger and nodded.

I took a galvanising breath, wrenching my eyes away from her body and focused on her eyes.

"What happened to your horses?"

Her face creased with pain and for a second I regretted the question, unsure if it was because I could see the hurt it had caused, or because I'm afraid she'll end this game.

My entire body tingled with anticipation as she shifted on her chair, her forehead creasing with her thoughts.

When she finally spoke it was almost a whisper, "They were both shot." She inhaled deeply holding all of her emotions at bay, and I was raked with regret and desire; desire to take the pain away.

"Your reward?"

"I want you to kiss me." Her voice clipped.

I prowled over the bed and slid off the edge. My bare knees scraped against the worn carpet, but I didn't care; all that I cared about was the kiss. Her lips. Her warmth. I reached for her underwear and pulled them off. I could smell her arousal and my cock twitches, hungry and pained.

I reached for her knees and pulled them apart, forcing her ass to the edge of the chair, and I kissed her. The taste of her arousal was musky and delicious as my tongue swept around her. She moaned and her hand plunged into my hair, digging into my scalp. I was lost in the kiss, her flavour, her moans, and the feel of her thighs against my cheeks. And I knew I had to end it.

I forced myself away.

"That's not what I meant." Her voice was breathy and fiery.

"Then you should have been more specific." I licked my lips.

"Question four." She caught her breath, her cheeks flushed, her nipples erect, and her entire body quivering. I didn't want her to ask the next question because I was afraid it would be the one I won't be able to answer.

"No, still my turn." I could see she wanted to argue, so I kept talking. "Question two, where are your parents?"

Her face grew darker again and her answer was clipped. "They're on the farm." She was hiding something but she answered the question.

"Your reward?"

"I want you to touch me." She whispered.

I sank back to my knees before her and pushed myself up, bringing my hand to her neck. My knuckles brushed her chin, tracing her delicate bone structure. My hand fluttered open, and my fingers floated down her long neck, over her rounded clavicle, and to her pink puckered nipple. She shivered under my touch, and her whole body shimmered. My thumb traced her nipple, stroking leisurely back and forth in slow deliberate circles. My delicate strokes were relentless. She moaned, arching her back into my touch, and she pushed away against the chair as if she couldn't decide how much more she wanted, if anything at all. And still I stroked; watching her face, the bite of her lower lip, her fluttering eyelids, her desperate and needy moans. A circular, delicate torture. She was melting away, and all I wanted was more.

"Gabriel," My name a strangled moan. Her body shook under my touch, and I released her.

I sat back onto the bed, my erection painful and swollen. Her short breaths and lost composure threatened to push me over the edge.

"Ask me." Mia's breathless voice begged me.

"Question number three. Are your parents alive?"

Her eyes welled with tears, and she shook her head. I couldn't tell how raw the pain was—how fresh or deep—because she stood up and pushed my torso onto the bed, my legs hung over the side.

"My reward." Her mouth sank around my cock, and it was all I can do not to fall apart.

I groaned at the warmth. Her tongue flickered over me, and I shuddered at the sensation. "I won't last long." My voice was gritty and drenched in need.

She pulled away for an eternal instance. "I'm counting on it."

My hands clutched the sheet, and my knuckles turned white as her head dipped and her lips sucked. The heat of her mouth sending shivers down my spine. Her head bobbed and her breast danced around as she sank deeper and deeper around me. I groaned as I could feel the tension build up in my spine. Everything became harder, tighter, more desperate. And then she popped me out of her mouth. I growled in desperation, and Mia flicked her tongue over the head. I was feverish with need and tortured with the ache in my cock as she kept me on the edge. But the edge was coming. It was riding in like a wave, fast and furious, and there would be nothing that could stop it.

Her full, pouty lips closed on me once more, and this time there was no reprieve. Long and deep, she took me in and stroked my shaft. Electricity zapped in the head of my cock as her teeth grazed my skin.

"I can't hold on." I warned her, expecting her to retreat. Instead, she sucked deeper, harder, and faster. My entire core coiled, and my spine shuddered as I released myself into her mouth. Want and need, desire and hunger poured from me as I jerked and clutched and twisted. Still, she sucked and licked and remained in total control of me, my body, my undoing. I had never been so turned on and so exhilarated.

My heart raced and thumped as I reached for Mia. I wanted her on my mouth and on my body. I needed to share this with her. But instead, she pulled her hand away and licked her lips.

"Not till question number four."

I groaned in frustration.

Elation.

Confusion.

My senses frayed, my mind reeling.

"Mia…"

"Question four." She ensnared me with her brown eyes. "What did you mean last night? Why do you need to protect me? What is so dangerous? Where is all the pain coming from?"

My head fell back onto the bed, and I clenched my jaw. She asked and I would need to answer.

"Those are four questions." I stalled.

She bit her lower lip, and her eyes travelled the length of my body. My cock twitched at the heated look. Mia straddled me. The heat of her arousal against my groin.

"You're stalling." She slid along me, a slow measured movement, my cock responding.

"One question." I groaned.

"I need to know." Her hips rolled above me again. I reached for them, and she pushed my hands away.

"You're cheating," I growled as she clawed at my abdomen.

"So are you." I placed my hands back on her thighs, and this time she allowed me to guide her as she moved above me again. My cock rigid once more, I groaned at the feel of her against me.

"Answer me."

"Why? What difference would it make?"

"All the difference." She slid herself along my length, and my hand grazed her inner thigh.

She sucked in a breath but was undeterred.

"Pick one."

She bit her lower lip, and her body sank onto my hardness as she slid herself against me in a slow measured movement.

"Who are you afraid of?"

"You've changed the question."

"I've changed the rules." She rolled above me, pulling from me another agonised growl.

"That's not fair."

"Who said anything about being fair?" With another movement, my stomach coiled and the ache and need grew once again.

"I don't play with cheaters." I hissed and bucked, grabbing her arm and pulling her onto the bed. In a fluid motion, I was above her with my hips pinning her to the bed.

She yelped and bucked, but I pinned her hands beside her body and watched as her pink nipples danced; and her hair flew in frenzied waves; and her mouth rounded; and her cheeks flooded with pink. I wanted to sink so deep into her that I would embed myself there permanently. Leave a mark so deep, so feral that she would never be able to get rid of it.

"Gabriel, get off me."

"No."

"Gabriel."

"You cheated." My voice was so husky, she froze. I kissed her neck. "You bent the rules." I flicked a tongue over her nipple. "You're driving me insane." I ground my hips against her wetness and she moaned.

"Pick one question, Mia. That's all you're going to get out of me, because after I give you my answer I am going to claim my reward." My voice ached with want.

Mia's body trembled beneath me, her ragged breathing hissing through her mouth. "What pain, Gabriel? Tell me."

Shit.

Why did she pick that one?

Why did she ask any of them?

But, right then it didn't matter. She needed an answer, any answer, because I needed her.

"The pain of losing everything. Losing you."

"You can't lose me, Gabriel."

"I can't have you, Mia."

I didn't explain. I allowed myself to plunge into her, and she made the sweetest sound.

My mouth found hers and the sweet kisses were forgotten as heat seared through us both. Teeth clinking and tongues warring, our lips mashed together in a battle we both wanted to win, and we both needed to lose.

As she clawed and dug into my skin, I realised that sometime in the last few weeks she had become mine. Losing her would be the biggest pain I'd have to endure—harder than all of my shit-ass childhood, harsher than being at the mercy of Tony, more difficult than piling bodies and digging up graves. Losing Mia would scorch the very last pieces of humanity I had left. She would leave me bitter and angry and totally wrecked.

But keeping her was impossible. I would become obsessed by her, crazed and unhinged; and when they come to hurt her, so they could hurt me, I knew I would take desperate measures to keep her, to expose myself to her. And if I did, if I truly showed her what I was capable of and all I had done to possess the little I had, would she want to stay? If I showed her the monster, would she cover her eyes? Would she run?

Pain.

Wracking, agonising, torturous pain. Beautiful, infuriating, soft, angry pain.

I pushed into Mia again and again, her soft moans soothing the rising desperation.

"Gabriel." She called to me as her whole body writhed and shivered beneath me.

I pulled out and grabbed her waist, flipping her on to her belly. I didn't have to use words. Her body knew what mine needed, and she rose on her knees with her head thrust into the sheet.

I plunged into her depths, my fingers seeking out her wetness as the seed of our desire grew. The twisted ache sprouted into salacious urgency, and I could feel that her desire matched mine—the need—in the way that her mouth pouted, and soft moans spilt from her lips. In the way her hands clawed at the sheet, white-knuckled. In the desperate way her hips crashed into my thrust, grinding against my finger—opening, bending, pushing, smashing, clashing.

Her body seized and screamed and, in a fit of moans, her pussy clenched and gripped and tugged at my cock. The ball of white-hot sensation lingered in my core, forcing me to pound against her, into her, through her. I reeled in the sound of her voice, battered against the feel of her skin, thrashed against the grip of her orgasm and, with a final hammering pulse, I groaned my release. The waves of her pleasure draining from me the last of my own as my insides already constricted with heartache.

I fell onto her back, my body smothering hers, covered in hot sweat and insatiable need.

I clutched onto her, clutched on to the idea of having her, and then I let go. I rolled over onto my back and tried to remember how to breathe.

Mia turned to me, her head resting on my chest her hand twirling in the patch of hair there. We lay silent.

Absorbing.

Accepting.

Sinking.

Drowning.

"Gabriel?"

"Yeah." My hand found her spine, and I trailed the delicate skin.

"What do you mean you can't have me?"

I took a galvanising breath. My hand plunged into her hair and tugged at the strands, forcing her to look at me. But instead of talk, I found her lips—red and raw, soft and inviting, sucking and tugging.

When I pulled away, I feared it might be for the last time.

"There are people who don't like the fact that I've come to acquire this place or the method by which I did. There are people who question how and why I'm here and, these people, they're not good people."

"Gabriel..." I raised a hand to silence her.

"They've tried to hurt me before, and they'll probably do it again. And if they know," I raked a hand through my hair, "If they sense, if they think, if they get a whiff of the feelings I have for you, you *will* become a weapon to use against me. You *will* be in danger because of me. You *will* get hurt, and I won't be able to bear that mark."

"Gabriel..."

"Don't."

"I'm not afraid of them."

"Then you're being stupid. This isn't a game where the rules can be bent. This isn't a game at all. It's real and it's fucking petrifying."

"My feeling for you are also real." Her voice raged with anger and hurt.

I rolled off the bed and stood up, running my palms along my face.

"You said everything was legal, above board." Her tone was scathing, broken.

"I didn't lie"

"So why are they after you?"

"The game is over, Mia. No more questions."

"I thought this wasn't a game."

"It's not!"

"Then why won't you answer me?"

"Because it's none of your fucking business." I sighed. My chest rose and fell with angry breaths.

"Don't." It was so soft, so full of anguish.

"Don't what?"

"Don't shut me out. Don't believe that you're not good enough. You are. You are good, I've seen it. You deserved to be loved."

I scoffed at her. "I'm not looking for love. I'm not looking for anything."

She stood from the bed and reached for me, her neck craned and her swollen eyes searching mine. "Why are you doing this?"

Why?

Because I knew how much she meant to me already, how dangerous it was, how much I needed to be entwined in her and never let go. Like a vine that climbs a fence and grows and spreads until it suffocates it, that's what I would do. My love would be all consuming. I would be selfish, and all I would want is to possess her, to own what's mine, to protect it at all costs. Loving her would be the most exquisite form of self-destruction.

The silence of my thoughts stretched as my heart ricochet in my chest.

"You put up walls, thinking you're strong. But, really, they just hold you back from experiencing so many beautiful things." Her voice cracked. "I can't fix you, and I don't want to; that's an inside job, Gabriel."

She placed her hands on my chest, pushing against the skin, searching for a heart that was already in pieces.

She searched my face, maybe for softness, maybe a crack in my resolve. "I'll stay if you just say that you'll try. Let me over your walls."

"You don't want to see over the wall. You want to break them all down."

"And, what's wrong with that?"

I ran my hands over my face. Everything—why couldn't she see?

"We can't be together."

"Yes, we can."

"I won't put you in danger."

"That's not your call to make."

"I've already made it."

"Fuck you, Gabriel."

"You just did." I smiled at her, a cocky asshat grin

The slap came out of nowhere; I can't say it was unexpected, but it stung deeper and longer than it should have.

Her wild hair swayed about her as she pulled on her shirt and found her underwear. She slammed her legs through the holes and retrieved her skirt. She was dressed too fast. Everything was happening too fast. Her angry eyes stared blankly, cold and swollen with humiliation. Her face red, and her hands shaking.

I went too far. Or maybe not far enough.

She marched out of my room, letting the door slam shut followed a few seconds later by the reverberating bang of the heavy iron door.

My body already ached at the memory of her touch, as I was swallowed by the silence. Drenched in sweat and guilt, my fists pounded the bed. I raked slow fingers across my face, my teeth grinding as they held my screams captive.

She just told me her parents died, and I sent her home crying, telling her all I was after was a cheap fuck.

I fell back onto my bed, lying there like a dead man—a corpse whose heart had stopped beating, a ravaged, collapsing carcass of a man. She deserved so much better.

Everything slowed as I fell from the bed and dressed. I didn't want to shower or brush my teeth. I didn't want to wash away what she had left behind—her smell, her taste, her echoing warmth—I may never shower again, not until the musk would turn into a stink. As always, I took something beautiful and crushed it.

By the time I reached Simone's, I had rebuilt the walls—cold, hard, and impenetrable. Spots came rushing over and stopped as if sensing a change, a break; a sorrow buried so deep that only his nose could find it, like a corpse buried six feet under.

He didn't leap or run home. Spots walked by my side, his head turning up at me, his watery eyes flickering questioning looks.

"She'll be back on Monday. For work." He wagged his tail.

———

My head throbbed and the light seared through my retinas. I swung my legs over the side of the bed kicking the cold glass. It clinked and rolled.

I fell to my knees and dug the bottle from under the bed. I fumbled with the cap and sipped on the last few drops of whiskey. The drink sloshed down my throat, burning all the way down. I tossed the empty bottle away and pulled myself up.

My stomach lurched in protest, and I ignored it. I've been hungry before. Anyway, a liquid diet was still a diet. Substituting alcohol with food was a real thing. Beer had yeast and bread had yeast; by that comparison I'd had over twenty-four sandwiches in the last twenty-four hours. The whiskey was just the dessert.

I pissed, barely holding myself up and ran a hand over my face. A day and a half of growth bristled against my palm. I washed my hands and splashed some water on my face. Nothing was going to fix the dark circles or sunken skin.

I ran my wet hand over my bed hair and brushed my teeth. I had already washed away her taste. The alcohol like a disinfectant eroding her away from my system. I pulled on my work jeans and a black shirt and stepped into the workshop. Everything was too bright and too loud. The boys were already working. I looked at the time. Just after ten. Shit.

I looked up at the office. Mia wasn't there. My jaw

clenched as the shrill of the phone cut across the workshop. It must have rang twenty times before it fell silent again.

My eyes wrenched themselves from the office windows. Maybe they thought that by staring Mia would appear. I could feel eyes on me, and I turned to see Romeo and Leo staring at me.

"She didn't come this morning." Leo's tone was cautious.

"Yeah, no shit." My voice was gritty and coarse and the alcohol leached from every pore. "Get back to work."

I wobbled up the stairs and went into the office. Everything was untouched since Saturday night. The chair pushed against the wall. The desk meticulous, minus a singular whiskey tumbler that held an inch of water.

I grabbed the glass and threw some ice into it. I poured a generous portion of whiskey from the decanter and gulped. The alcohol rushed through my veins and steadied my nerves. The phone rang again.

I let it.

When it had fallen silent, I picked up the receiver and called Mia's number.

Voicemail.

I tried again.

And again

And again

After the sixth time, I threw the phone across the room. It exploded against the tempered window, which imploded in veins that spread across the length of the pane. I stared at the cracks like I was looking at a window to my soul. I stormed down the stairs. "I'm going out," I called after me, as I exited through the open roller door.

I arrived at her apartment and knocked on the door. Nothing.

I pounded on her door. "Mia," I called as I continued pounding. "Open the door." Alcohol and rage were not a good mix for me

I waited. Listened. Wondered.

But she was gone.

I sank to the floor, leaning against the door, my stomach growling, and suddenly I was six again and waiting to wake the fuck up.

To be continued...

ACKNOWLEDGMENTS

A Word from Jane:

I would like to start by thanking you, the reader, so much for reading! If you enjoyed the story, please leave a review and recommend the book to any friend you think would love Gabriel's story. You will have my eternal love and gratitude. Even a few short words go a long way.

As always, I would love to thank my wonderful friend and beta Dawn, her enthusiasm knows no boundaries, her genuine love for books, reading, and helping authors is contagious and humbling. I have loved having her in my corner. Thank you.

To all my other betas and C/Ps your input and critiques have been invaluable, without you Gabriel would not have been where he is today."

ABOUT THE AUTHOR

Jane Wynters doesn't quite know how to answer the question of "where are you from?" She's moved from place to place like a snowflake on the wind always searching for a safe place to land. She loves meeting new people and exploring new places. She loves reading, writing and conjuring new worlds from her imagination. Coffee is at the top of her food pyramid and she is fluent in three languages, her favourite being sarcasm.

Want to know more about the author and keep in touch? Get snippets of up coming books and have a bit of twisted fun?

Come join me in Wonderland…

If you enjoyed Gabriel's beginning, why not leave a review and tell everyone how much you enjoyed Spare Parts?

www.ingramcontent.com/pod-product-compliance
Lightning Source LLC
Chambersburg PA
CBHW030648110726
47901CB00002B/615